The Gaia Solution

The Gaia Collection Book 3

Claire Buss

Published by CB Visions in 2019

First Edition

www.cbvisions.weebly.com

Cover artwork by Ian Bristow

Other works by Claire Buss:

The Gaia Collection
The Gaia Effect
The Gaia Project
The Gaia Solution

The Roshaven Books
The Rose Thief
The Interspecies Poker Tournament – The Roshaven Case Files No. 27
Ye Olde Magick Shoppe

Poetry
Little Book of Verse, Book 1 of the Little Book Series
Little Book of Spring, Book 2 of the Little Book Series
Little Book of Summer, Book 3 of the Little Book Series
Spooky Little Book, Book 4 of the Little Book Series

Short Story Collections
Tales from Suburbia
Tales from the Seaside
The Blue Serpent & other tales
Flashing Here and There

Anthologies
Underground Scratchings, Tales from the Underground anthology
Patient Data, The Quantum Soul anthology
A Badger Christmas Carol, The Sparkly Badgers' Christmas Anthology
Dress Like An Animal and Afraid of the Dark, Haunted, the Sparkly Badgers' Anthology

Our story is set two-hundred years in the future after much of the planet and the human race have been decimated during The Event, when the world went to war with high-energy radiation weapons.

In The Gaia Effect, Kira and Jed Jenkins – a young couple who were recently allocated a child – together with their closest friends, discover Corporation have been deliberately lying to them and forcing them to remain sterile. With help from Gaia, the spirit of the Earth, the group of friends begin to fight back against Corporation eventually winning and taking over the governance of City 42.

In The Gaia Project, Corporation fight back under a new, more terrifying organization called New Corp and Kira, Jed and their friends end up fleeing for their lives trying to find a safe place to live. They travel to City 36 and City 9 in vain and must go further afield.

We join them on their journey into the unknown.

Chapter One

'We shouldn't have left them,' muttered Kira as she looked out of the plane window. They were heading for the Resistance base, across the ocean, away from her island. She could make out several drones buzzing around Artem's compound where they had left her parents, Ruth and baby Sarah, and the rest of the Force soldiers. She squinted. It looked like a convoy of skimmers was heading towards the buildings.

'Artem says they will be well protected, hon. He told me about several security measures he has in place. New Corp won't try anything, they don't have the firepower to win.' Jed tried to reassure his wife, but he too felt uneasy. Who really knew what New Corp had at their disposal?

'But my mum is down there. And dad. And Ruth and Sarah. It doesn't feel right.'

'They didn't want to come with us, Kira. And to be honest, I can't blame them. Your mum needs to rest, she needs the medicine Artem has, and as for Ruth, I think it's better for her to stay.' Jed glanced out the plane window. 'You know, we probably should've left the other children there as well. Safer there than here.' At that moment, the plane hit a pocket of turbulence and bounced its passengers around. Jed chuckled nervously as he gripped the arm rests.

Everyone, apart from Zac, was nervous about flying. No-one, apart from Zac, had flown before.

A loud boom made them both jump and look out of the window again.

'NO!' screamed Kira. 'Stop the plane, stop the fragging plane.' She scrabbled with the seat belt, trying to get out of her seat before her fingers had managed to undo the clasp. 'We have to go back! WE HAVE TO GO BACK!'

Her manic response frightened the children, Grace and Peter. They began screaming which woke Lucas who had been sleeping peacefully next to Martha. The three babies fed into each other's dismay, their cries growing louder and louder. Ash unclipped his seatbelt and hurried over to try and soothe Grace and Peter while darting shocked glances out the window.

Jed stared in disbelief at the smoke and flames rising from the ground below. Artem's complex had been destroyed. Jed was frozen, unable to move or speak. In his head he was back in City 42, staring at a pale arm sticking out from the rubble of Corp Tech. His chest constricted and he couldn't breathe. Kira's frantic screams had faded into the background, his ears were deafened by rushing blood. Bile rose up his throat as he shook his head to try and clear his thoughts.

Max was banging on the pilot's door, demanding that they open the cockpit. A confused looking Zac appeared.

'What's wrong, Max?' Zac's eyes darted to the other passengers, frowning in confusion at the screams of anguish coming from Kira and the crying children.

'They've blown the complex up. We have to go back.'

'What?' Zac couldn't comprehend what Max was trying to tell him. He ducked his head to look out of one of the side windows and saw the huge plume of black smoke. He stared blankly for a moment then clenched his jaw before going back into the cockpit, letting the door shut behind him.

Kira had finally managed to undo her seatbelt and rushed over to the door, pushing past Max. She started banging and shouting but there was no answer.

'Everyone, please, return to your seats. We cannot go back. We only go forwards. If New Corp can destroy home, they can shoot down plane. I will get you to Resistance.' The mic crackled as Artem stopped talking.

Kira banged the door a few more times, sobbing before her legs gave way and she crumbled to the floor. Max looked beseechingly at Dina for some help. Together they tried to move her, but she was a dead weight. Dina wrapped her arms around her friend, trying to whisper words of comfort.

Martha, pale-faced and feeling shaky, stood up, her arms tightly wrapped around Lucas as she went to check on Jed. He still hadn't moved and was staring into nothing. She shifted the baby in her arms and put one hand on Jed's shoulder but there was no reaction.

'Jed? Jed, can you hear me?' Martha called to the others. 'I think he's in shock.' Then she dashed to the toilet, making it just in time as she threw up everything she had eaten that day.

At that moment, Zac came out of the cockpit, stopping briefly to make sure Max and Dina were alright before stepping over Kira and hurrying to be with Martha.

'Are you okay?' He put a comforting arm on her back.

'Am I okay? After New Corp just blew up my friend...' Martha's bottom lip wobbled, and a sharp cry escaped. She leaned back into Zac's arms, her shoulders shaking as she wept. The little boy in her arms confused about what was happening.

'Compound report, over.' Artem tried to hail a member of his staff on the plane's radio but there was no reply. Nothing but static. He checked the plane's fuel gauges; they were half full. He could risk banking right and circling around to see what had happened. 'Everyone, hold tight.' Artem's voice came over the intercom as he banked the plane.

Max stumbled in the aisle but managed to flop into an empty chair. Dina and Kira were wedged together in the aisle and Jed had never left his seat, but Martha, Lucas and Zac tipped into the open toilet cubicle.

'Ow!'

'Are you okay?'

'Just get off us.' Martha pushed Zac away. 'What the frag is going on?'

'Artem is circling back to see what happened,' called Max. 'You'd better buckle up. We don't know what we're getting into.'

Martha pushed past Zac, her face red from crying. She clipped herself and Lucas into a seat, ignoring everything else.

Zac frowned at her as he stalked past, going back to the cockpit. He had only been trying to help.

'How's it looking, Artem?' Zac asked as he plugged himself back into the co-pilot controls.

'There is... nothing.'

Zac and Artem looked out the window at rubble and smoke. The entire compound had been destroyed.

'Do you think anyone made it?' Zac was scanning the

scene for any signs of life.

'With warning, maybe. I have bunker. But this, this was attack from nowhere. My Ruth and little one... gone.' Artem's hands tightened on the pilot controls turning his knuckles white. 'They will pay for this.' He increased the throttle, sweeping the plane round in a full arc, accelerating away from the attack zone. 'They will pay.'

A second boom filled the skies as Artem's supply of biogas ignited. The plane shuddered, caught in the blast radius but their course held steady. The continual noise and turbulence pulled Jed out of his nonresponsive state.

'What happened? Kira? Where's Kira?' He panicked, the plaintive cries of his children confusing him further.

'She's here,' Max called and waved from the front of the plane to get Jed's attention. 'She's here, on the floor.'

Jed noticed Ash crouched down next to Grace and Peter and clapped one grateful hand on the man's shoulder as he fumbled one-handed, trying to undo his seat belt. Finally free, he hurried over to Max. Dina looked up at him with a tear stained face.

'I heard what they said in the cockpit. There's nothing left.'

But Jed didn't know what to say in response. None of them did.

'Kira? Kira, hon? Can you stand?' Jed reached out for his wife and she grabbed his hand, squeezing it tight. He pulled her upright and guided her back to their seats. She clung onto him, stumbling as she shuffled across the plane's causeway. Grace lifted her arms when she saw her mum, but Kira didn't register her. Ash did his best to distract the confused little girl.

'I'll make some synth-caf, extra sugar, for the shock.' Max didn't know what else to do but he wanted to do something.

'I'll help,' said Dina, looking for anything to take her mind off what they had witnessed.

'What happened, Jed?' Kira's voice was shaky.

'New Corp must have struck Artem's compound.'

'Because they thought we were there?'

'I suppose.' Jed couldn't quite believe it himself.

'So, we killed them. We killed all those people and Ruth and Sarah and my mum and dad. Oh, oh, Jed, we killed my parents! And Sarah, she's not even Grace's age and we killed her. We just left them all to die. How could you? HOW COULD YOU?' Kira was screaming and hitting her husband in rage and grief.

Jed withstood the blows, knowing there was nothing he could say or do right now to help his wife. He held her loosely as the punches began to lose their potency and the sobs became louder. He was struggling to comprehend how the attack had happened let alone the fact that Kira had lost her parents, one of her closest friends and a baby had died. Not to mention all the Force operatives he'd left behind and the soldiers and staff Artem had had at the compound.

Max and Dina handed out the hot drinks. Involuntarily Jed took a sip then winced at the sweetness but dutifully drank the whole cup and it did calm the jitters he had been feeling inside. Martha was holding Lucas tightly, rocking back and forth - more to comfort herself than the child who had no idea what had happened. Dina and Max sat a couple of rows over, ashen faces, hands clasped around their mugs of synth-caf, disbelief etched on their face. Jed looked to his daughter Grace and his nephew Peter. They had both calmed down. The initial turbulence and reaction to the explosion had frightened them both badly but Ash had stepped in and distracted the children with silly faces and biscuits. Jed mouthed a silent thank you at his second-in-command.

Kira had quietened now. She pushed her hair away from her face and wiped her eyes, sniffing loudly. Seeing Ash crouched nearby and entertaining the kids, she half-fell out of her chair in her haste to check on them herself. Her abrupt movements startled the kids, but they didn't cry, just regarded her with big, wide eyes. She knelt in front of them, giving them both a kiss and trying to smile.

'Mum-mum,' gurgled Grace, holding out a small, chubby hand.

'Yes, it's mum-mum, darling.' Kira's voice wavered as she thought about her mum, but she cleared her throat and in a wobbly voice asked them if they wanted to choose something else to eat. Ash stood up and moved out of her way.

'Do you think she's alright?' Jed asked him.

Both of them watched Kira for a moment.

'I don't think any of us are,' replied Ash in a soft voice.

Jed nodded. He had expected the rage and the tears but trying to put a brave face on everything was not like his wife. He was worried. 'Do you know how much longer the flight is?'

'A couple of hours I think, maybe a bit longer after that circling back. The best thing any of us can do now is try and get some rest.' Ash patted Jed on the shoulder. He started opening the overhead lockers looking for blankets and pillows to hand out to everyone.

An odd silence fell over the group. Even the children were quiet. The friends sat apart, each trying to work through their initial shock and grief.

Once the children were asleep, Kira lay back in her chair, staring blindly out of the plane's window. She'd just lost both her parents and her first reaction was to turn to her mum to figure out how to deal with such grief and every time she thought about doing that, it was like another blow to her body because her mum wasn't there anymore.

'Do you think...?' Kira turned to Jed, to try and ask him whether he thought there was any chance her parents had survived but he had fallen asleep. She watched him sleep, a slight frown in his forehead, the only sign that things weren't as they should be.

Unable to sleep, Kira longed for the flight to end and for the plane to touch down. Eventually there was a crackle on the intercom.

'We have arrived. Please, keep seatbelts on and remain seated until plane has touched down and we are parked in hangar.' Artem's voice lacked its usual vitality, matching the feeling of despair the rest of the passengers were feeling. No-one spoke as the plane came to a standstill or when Zac came out of the cabin to open the doors of the plane and extend the stairs.

'Um. There should be someone to meet us, they'll get the bulk of your belongings brought in so no need to worry about those. Just bring what you need now, the essentials. Are you ready?' His gaze flicked from person to person. He seemed nervous.

Martha was the first to stand. She had her bag slung across her body and Lucas held tightly on one hip. She stalked down the gangway and out into the night air. Zac hurried after her.

'Do you need any help?' Dina asked as she hovered next to Kira's chair.

'Can you take Peter, please?' Kira's voice was

unemotional. She moved mechanically, checking they hadn't forgotten anything before taking Grace out of her seat and carrying her own bag.

Dina picked up Peter and shrugged slightly at Max as she followed Kira out of the plane.

'Sir? Are you ready to leave the plane?'

Jed flinched in his seat at hearing Ash's voice.

'Yes. Let's go,' he said, standing up and grabbing his own bag.

Max clapped Ash on the back as the men exited. Hearing someone address him as a superior had given Jed the momentum he needed to get moving. He knew the full force of grief would soon hit them all but for now they needed to keep moving.

Once outside, Jed activated the cube strollers they had brought with them from the island for the children. Martha decided to keep hold of Lucas, but Kira gratefully placed Grace inside and Peter was eager to join his cousin. The children were excited at being off the plane and were cooing with interest.

Artem was the last to leave. There was no point in him flying back to his compound. It didn't exist anymore. He had made sure all the controls had been turned off and closed the exit behind him. The plane looked lonely in the empty hangar bay. He patted the bodywork fondly as he locked up and looked for the others who were gathered uncertainly behind Zac.

Chapter Two

'General Ridgley. Glad to have you back, Sir.' A smartly turned out woman in a khaki jumpsuit saluted Zac as the group walked towards her, stopping by the hangar bay doors. 'What happened? We had reports of an explosion on the island?'

General? mouthed Dina to Max who shrugged. She looked at Artem. 'Did you know?' she whispered.

'Da. Is fine.' The big Russian grinned at them but Dina tutted at him.

'You could have said something,' she hissed at him but was interrupted by Zac speaking.

'Thank you, Colonel Archer. Good to be back.' Zac glanced back briefly at the others but made no explanations. 'Artem's compound was attacked and destroyed.' He let out a breath. 'We were lucky to get out in one piece. What's the latest report here?'

Colonel Archer cast a doubtful eye over the odd group of civilians stood with him.

'It's alright, Colonel. You can speak freely. I vouch for all of them,' said Zac firmly as he started to walk out of the hangar.

Everyone hurried to keep up while at the same time looking around them to see where they were. There wasn't much to see. The airstrip was empty and there were a few buildings in the distance. Archer and Zac led them along a marked path for pedestrians, leading them away from the runway, towards a security fence and the buildings.

'Yes, Sir. We've had three new groups of refugees arrive and have been able to update the cities file accordingly. Together with the information you and Misner were able to provide we have an up to date indication of the strength of New Corp.'

'Anything else?'

'Yes, Sir. There have been some developments in the environmental scans. Humphries is waiting to give you a full debrief.'

'Very good, Colonel. Please escort our guests to the base and see that they are made comfortable.' He nodded at the Russian. 'Artem, please, you are welcome here as well.' Zac finally spoke directly to Martha. 'I'll join you and the others as soon as I can. And I'll explain everything.' He half smiled at her before walking swiftly away from them, towards a waiting skimmer, on the other side of the security fence.

Martha could feel all eyes on her, but she did not know what to say. Colonel Archer came to the rescue.

'Welcome to the Resistance. I'm Colonel Archer and I will escort you to your quarters.'

Nobody replied.

Archer tried again. 'Look, I'm sorry for the circumstances that brought you here, especially if you lost someone. We've all lost people here. But the Resistance will welcome you, if you choose to join us.'

'Are we free to leave?' asked Dina bluntly.

Archer regarded her for a moment before replying. 'There's nowhere to go.' And she walked away.

Artem was already moving and whistling as if nothing had happened. Nobody else knew what to say in response and the rest of the group unwillingly followed as Archer led them through the gate in the security fence. They walked half the length of the airstrip before they arrived at several squat, red brick buildings. A few soldiers were running drills to the right of them and Martha spied the skimmer Zac had taken over to the left. It was parked and empty. She tried to think what was important for her to notice but a blue light caught her attention in the corner of her left eye. She turned her head and stopped walking abruptly. Shimmering in the distance was Gaia.

Dina bumped into her, breaking Martha's line of sight but she grabbed Dina's arm excitedly and pointed.

'Look! Look! Did you see her?'

The others looked confused because there was nothing there. Colonel Archer turned back to find out what the delay was.

'See what?' she asked.

Martha ignored her, turning instead to Kira. 'Did you see her? Gaia? She was just there?'

Kira stared in the direction Martha was pointing but there was nobody there. She shook her head at her friend and started pushing the cube stroller again, closing the gap between her and the colonel.

Dina patted Martha on the arm as she walked by.

'I did see her. I did.' But Martha was talking to no-one. Casting another look in the direction she'd seen the blue lady, she sighed in frustration. 'I did.'

'Wait here,' ordered Archer as she took them through an external door into a small waiting room. She waved her wrist at a security panel and another door swished open for her, closing quickly behind.

'Implants,' explained Artem as he took one of the seats.

'You don't have one?' asked Dina, taking the chair next to him.

'I am not official member of Resistance. I fly plane now and then but always I go back.' He tried to smile at her. 'Now, I don't know.'

Dina smiled back sadly and watched the others. Kira had Peter and Grace in a double cube. Both children were stood up, looking around interestedly and holding onto the cube sides. They wouldn't be able to climb out, but they had a good view of everything. Martha still held Lucas. There was another collapsible cube in her bag, but she hadn't activated it yet preferring instead to hold her son. Dina couldn't blame her. Sarah used to share that cube with Lucas. She grabbed Max's hand as he stood next to her, squeezing it tight.

Max looked down at his girlfriend and gave her a quick smile. He was uneasy. It was taking Colonel Archer an awfully long time to come back from wherever it was she had gone.

The door opened.

A second soldier, dressed in the same khaki jumpsuit, followed Archer out of the doors. He was short with close-cropped hair and thick glasses that he adjusted nervously as everyone stared at him.

'This is Lieutenant Kolwowsky. He'll inject you with one of our security chips then you'll be able to open doors and access the medical and food supplies. It doesn't hurt,' said Archer and she waited for someone to volunteer.

No-one came forward. Kira looked at Jed for reassurance while Max and Dina shrugged at each other. Martha was waiting for someone else to go first while

Artem looked on in amusement. But before he could speak Ash stood up.

'Er... I'll go first?' he volunteered, holding out his left arm.

Jed frowned at him for being so quick to comply making Ash falter.

'Is this really necessary?' Jed asked Archer.

'It is if you want access to the base. Everyone here has one,' she replied.

'What about the children?' asked Martha in concern, holding Lucas even closer to her.

'Um...' For the first time Archer looked unsure. She glanced at Kolwowsky for help.

'We don't have any babies here but all our children have a chip so they can get to school, in and out of the mess hall, that sort of thing. It's perfectly safe, I promise.' He smiled encouragingly at them.

Jed nodded once and Ash stepped forward again. Kolwowsky grinned as he moved closer with his med-gun. A quick stab in the arm and the chip was embedded. He turned to Max and Dina who were stood nearby and waited for them to roll up their sleeves.

'Is this so you can keep an eye on us?' asked Martha, eyeing the med-gun doubtfully as Kolwowsky came to administer her chip and one for Lucas. The little boy didn't even murmur at the injection.

'The chip does have tracking capability but that's not such a bad thing when there's nothing but desert outside of our dome, ' replied Archer.

'This place is domed?' Max looked out of the window in surprise, he hadn't noticed the tell-tale shimmer.

'Yep, new tech developed right here,' Kolwowsky replied. 'We aim to find better ways to get things done here.'

'Thank you, Lieutenant. That will be all.' Archer raised an eyebrow at the soldier as he threw her a cheeky grin alongside a salute, going back the way he had come.

'If you will follow me, I'll take you to your barracks. It's not much but you won't be disturbed, and we've put you all together.' She waved her arm at the doors to open them and gestured for the group to proceed her down the corridor.

'I don't like this, Jed. We could be walking into anything,' muttered Kira as they passed by several doors but no signs of other people.

'Let's just wait and see, hon. Wait and see.'

'Artem better have an explanation for how this happened,' Kira said bitterly.

'It wasn't his fault. We couldn't have known New Corp would attack. I think we were lucky to get away.'

Kira glowered at him but said nothing. Her parents were dead. Ruth and her little girl were dead. There was no luck in any of that.

Archer led them to the end of the corridor and stopped in front of a set of double doors. 'This is you,' she gestured.

Dina went first, feeling silly as she opened the doors with a wave of her arm. The others followed her inside. The doors led into a communal area with a few sofas and a small kitchen. There were more doors on the righthand side. Dina opened the nearest and revealed a small bedroom with two single beds and a small set of drawers for personal items.

Kira opened another to reveal the same layout.

'There's enough space for all of you. I'll leave you to settle in. Someone will be along soon with your belongings. There are some supplies in the cupboards, but we all eat our main meals together in the communal mess hall at the other end of the corridor. Dinner is at 1800 hours. If you need anything, you can reach Lieutenant Kolwowsky on line one.' She tossed a couple of two-way radios onto the table.

'That's a bit old school, isn't it?' commented Max.

'We make the most of everything available to us here at the Resistance.' Archer gave a brief smile before leaving. The doors slid closed behind her.

There was silence as the group looked around them.

'I'll make some synth-caf,' announced Kira, unpacking a pouch she had in her hand luggage and going in search of mugs in the small kitchen.

Martha expanded the cube Grace and Peter were in, turning on its entertainment capabilities and putting Lucas in with the other children. She joined Kira in the kitchen area and soon there were several cups of steaming synth-caf circulating the group.

Chapter Three

Zac stood in his office and scanned the briefing file in front of him, looking up briefly as Colonel Archer arrived. He was aware of her standing to his left but said nothing as he finished looking over the report.

'Not what we'd hoped, Archer.'

'No, Sir. Fewer groups of refugees are arriving. I don't think there will be many more. We can clear cities 24, 30 and 11 from the board. They're not viable.'

Zac glanced at the map on the wall. It was accurate as they had been able to make it. Everyone who arrived was questioned carefully to determine which city they came from, which cities they'd passed and other important environmental information.

'You can take 36 off the map, as well as 15.'

'Were they both destroyed by New Corp?'

'No. 36 is full of radiation, it won't be safe to inhabit for decades to come. Shame really, a stronghold in the mountains would have been a tactical advantage.'

'Not when you read the latest report, Sir.' Archer bit her lip as she waited for her superior to catch up on the results of weeks of investigation. She caught herself tapping her fingers impatiently and held back the urge to speak before he'd finished reading. Finally, Zac put the handheld down and leaned heavily on the desk in front of him.

'The entire country?'

'That's what it looks like, Sir.'

'And the calculations are correct?'

'To the best of our knowledge.' Archer paused. 'Who are the people you brought with you, Sir?'

Zac pushed himself to standing and began ticking names off his fingers. 'Artem you know. From City 42 we have their former rebel leader, Martha Hamble with her son as well as Archivist Kira Jenkins and former Force detective Jed Jenkins with their children. Dr Max Carter and Dina Grey are scientists, originally from Camp Eden, and Ash is one of Jed's men.'

'Perhaps their scientists can independently verify the data for us. It might also make them join our cause, when they know some of the facts.'

'I don't think we need to worry about whether they will join or not. None of them are pro New Corp.'

'How do you know, Sir?'

Zac closed down his info wall.

'New Corp wiped out Artem's complex...'

'Yes, we know that, Sir.' Archer interrupted.

'Kira's parents were there. As was one of the new mothers from City 42. With her child.'

Wide-eyed, Archer paled and took a step back.

'Are they all... dead?'

'Completely annihilated. I don't think we need to be worried about them being motivated to help us. We might have to hold them back.' Zac gestured at the discarded handheld on the table. 'Make sure they get a copy of your latest report. I want them to have all the facts.'

'Not redacted?'

'No, Archer. There's no time for secrets. We need to pull together and find a solution, fast. Dismissed.'

Archer saluted and they went their separate ways. Although he hadn't shown it to Archer, Zac was shaken by what had happened to Artem's compound and all he could think of was finding Martha and making sure she was alright.

Dina was exploring the quarters they had been assigned. There was no sign of previous occupancy and the food supplies were sparse. The info screen on the wall of the communal area began flashing, indicating a new message. Intrigued, Dina walked over and tapped the screen to access the information. She stopped reading after a few minutes.

'Guys! You'd better come and see this. Now!' she called to the others.

Kira and Martha looked up from the play cube where they had been half-heartedly entertaining the children. Jed, Max and Ash had been chatting in the kitchen area, refreshing their synth-caf. They all came to join Dina at the info screen.

'Read this.' Dina pointed and the screen and scrolled backwards to the beginning.

Field Report to Resistance Headquarters
The recent scientific expedition to our coastline has confirmed initial suspicions. Sea levels are rising, rapidly. Shoreline erosion has increased, and internal waterways are flooding up and down the country. The pre-existing flood works near the coast are now redundant as they reside several metres below water. The recommendation of this report is to find higher

ground, fast. We predict that the nearby island currently inhabited by New Corporation and its denizens will be underwater by the end of the year.

Martha stood in front of the screen, blocking the view to the others.

'Do you know what this means?'

Max nodded. 'Everyone we left behind will be drowned before the end of the year unless they can find a safe way off that island. If they've got their facts right, that is.'

'I doubt New Corp are planning to evacuate everyone. I didn't see any sign of any ships, just business as usual in City 9,' commented Jed.

'They must have some kind of plan, there's no way New Corp would allow themselves to perish,' argued Kira.

'You're right. New Corp won't perish. The people in charge left the island several months ago. One final management level remains but I doubt they'll be there long. New Corp control cities 42 and 9 remotely from headquarters we have been unable to find. Yet.' Zac spoke confidently but he scanned the group, looking for signs of friendliness or hostility.

'You knew New Corp had the firepower to destroy Artem's compound, didn't you?' Kira accused Zac.

'Not exactly.'

'What the frag does that mean?' exploded Jed.

Zac raised his arms in surrender. 'It means, we thought they might have the fire power, but we didn't know they were ready to use it.' He looked directly at Kira. 'I had no idea they would attack. I am so, so very sorry for your loss.'

Kira gave a curt nod and turned away, unwilling to

share her grief with him.

'And what about you, Zac? Did your parents really own that museum? Was it all a cover? Why were you even there?' Martha was angry.

'My aunt and uncle, who practically raised me so yes, that bit is true. But it was also a convenient cover to spy on New Corp's communication network and try to figure out what their plans were. Being in City 9 was potentially a death sentence for anyone from the Resistance, which is why I was there.' He looked directly into her eyes. 'Sometimes a leader has to lead.'

Martha flushed and looked away, but the group weren't done with Zac yet.

'Why didn't you tell us you were the leader of the Resistance? Why the subterfuge?' Jed demanded. 'What else aren't you telling us?'

'Nothing. I've told Archer to give you full access to everything. Our whole camp, supplies and all our intel.' Zac took a deep breath. 'I need your help.'

Dina barked a laugh. 'What can we possibly help you with?'

Zac nodded towards the info screen. 'As you've read, we are on the verge of massive environmental upheaval, and I was hoping your connection to Gaia would help get us some answers on what to expect next.'

'Is that all?' asked Martha.

'Obviously we could use your scientific expertise and your understanding of anthropology. Your team has some unique skills, a fresh outlook and you're clearly problem solvers. Look at how you dealt with the clean water supply in City 42 - that was inspired thinking. We need your help. Will you stay?' Zac looked hopefully around the room.

It was Ash who spoke up this time.

'We need some time, to process all this. To grieve.'

'Of course. You can reach me on the comm. Anything you need, let my team know.' Zac paused. 'But I need to know your answer by morning. Time is something we don't have a lot of. We'll speak then.' He left them alone. It was a risky move, they could decide they were better off without getting involved in the Resistance, but after what had happened at Artem's, Zac was confident they would join the fight.

He needed them to.

Ash went to the door to make sure Zac had gone and that nobody else was nearby. The corridor was empty. He turned to the others.

'For what it's worth, I think we should pitch in. Helping them helps us,' he said.

'We don't know anything about where we are, who the people are, what's going on...' Dina trailed off.

'Exactly. We have no idea what's going on and he needs us. We have the upper hand here.' Ash looked to the others for confirmation. Martha was nodding but Kira looked pensive.

'How are we supposed to stop a world-wide environmental catastrophe?' she asked.

'You're the Gaia whisperer - ask for help I guess,' suggested Dina.

Kira put her head in her hands and spoke through her fingers. 'It doesn't work like that! It's not like I can just ping Gaia, you know.'

'It worked at Artem's...' Dina faltered. 'Where is Artem?'

'He said he needed some air, went for a walk I think,' replied Max. 'But Dina's right. You and Martha have had the most interaction with Gaia. She obviously feels deeply connected to you two. Maybe she will speak to you again, tell you what's going on. In her unique way.'

'I'd rather she just lay it out in black and white for all of us to understand,' muttered Jed.

'That would be too easy,' replied Kira with a small smile. 'I take it that means we're staying?' She looked at the others for confirmation. There were shared smiles and small nods. 'I know I feel safer here with the children then out there. For now, at least. We can rest here. Recuperate and plan what to do next. How we fight back. But first things first, we need to unpack.'

'Unpack what? Our bags haven't arrived yet!' grumbled Dina.

The door chimed and Kolwowsky appeared with an auto trolley, piled high with their bags. He stopped short at the sight of everyone staring at him and adjusted his glasses.

'Is everything alright?'

Max nodded and strode over. 'Let me help you with that.' He deftly took over the controls and steered the trolley towards the back of the communal area where the bedrooms were located.

'Can I get you anything else? Will you be joining us for dinner?' Kolwowsky asked hopefully.

'Yes. What time and where do we need to go?' asked Jed, he'd forgotten what Archer had told them.

'Dinner is at 1800 hours. Here's a map of the base.' Kolwowsky tapped their info screen as he was talking and pointed to a collection of purple dots. 'This is you. You can change the settings to search for people, but I figured it would more straightforward to show you where you are to start with.' He dragged a finger across the screen to a large area highlighted yellow. 'This is the mess hall.' Looking up, he grinned at Jed. 'I'll see you there. If you need anything else before then, let me know.' He adjusted his glasses again before smiling and leaving.

'Helpful, aren't they?' Martha remarked.

'A little too keen,' said Kira.

'Let's go to dinner and see what the vibe is like. The Resistance might be what we've been looking for.' Dina was looking forward to finding out more.

Chapter Four

They heard the mess hall before they found it. A cacophony that only grew louder as they entered. Long rows of tables with bench seating were laid out parallel to each other. Other people were entering and leaving the mess hall through the doors behind Kira, Jed and the others and at first no-one noticed them, but then Lucas started to cry, frightened by the loud noise.

Instantly heads swivelled at the sound of a child crying. Kira scanned the crowd, there were some young children but none of them were younger than about five or six. There were no other babies. She inched closer to Jed, holding Grace tightly with one arm, and found her husband's free hand, grasping it tightly. Jed held onto Peter with his other arm and squeezed Kira's hand in mutual support.

'Hi! Hey, over here!' It was Kolwowsky waving at them. He'd secured the end of one of the tables with enough seating for them all to sit together.

On closer inspection Kira noticed the food was already on the tables; her stomach rumbled as the smell of what looked like stew hit her nose. She was hungrier than she'd imagined.

As they sat down the conversation levels in the room

began to rise again, the topic of discussion almost exclusively the new arrivals. Martha had managed to soothe Lucas enough to stop him crying but he clung to her tightly. She fumbled in her bag for a bottle of milk and smiled gratefully at Dina who came to her rescue. As Martha fed her son, Dina spooned out some of the stew for her and grabbed a hunk of bread. There were carafes of water on the table and empty glasses, so Max poured for everyone.

Kira shared small pieces of bread with Grace while Jed fed Peter. The others tucked in, no-one saying a word as they focused on eating. It was delicious and clearly not rehydrated food sachets.

'We grow everything in our allotments,' said Kolwowsky, grinning at them as everyone enjoyed their food. 'How are you settling in?'

'Okay, thanks,' replied Dina. She'd finished first. 'There isn't much in the fridge though, can we get some more supplies from somewhere?'

'Sure. I'll take you to Stores when you're finished here. You'll have to sign for what you want - the internal AI system monitors who has what preventing hoarding and ensuring there is enough for everyone.'

'Internal AI system?' Ash interrupted. 'Is it interactive? Can I see it in action?'

Kolwowsky laughed. 'It's just a Stores system, but sure, you can see it in action. We call it Frank.'

'Excellent,' replied Ash. He turned to Dina. 'I'll come with you to Stores, if that's alright?'

'Sure.' She was keen to see an AI system working as well.

'I'd like to take a look at your allotment if that's allowed?' asked Max. 'Part of my work at Camp Eden involved increasing crop yields. I might be able to lend a hand.'

Kolwowsky nodded enthusiastically around a mouthful of food. He cleared his throat. 'That would be great, we try and get everyone to pitch in round here and I know they're short handed over there. If you turn left out of here and follow the corridor all the way to the end, you'll reach the allotment. Bennett should be there; she will show you around. She's in charge of Allotment.'

'I will come too. Botany is my field of expertise after all,' said Martha.

Kolwowsky eyed the little boy on her lap who was looking wide-eyed at everything. 'What about him? I'm not sure it's really a safe space for children.'

'Do you actually have any creche facilities?' asked Kira.

'Er no, not really. There's a school for the kids but with today being Saturday there won't be any teachers around till Monday.' He leaned closer to the group. 'There aren't many babies in the Resistance. In fact, I think yours are the youngest children we have here.'

'I can keep hold of Lucas for you if you like, Ma. I'm not really in the mood to explore.' Kira felt tired. They had the play cube and individual sleeping cubes for each child. Being collapsible, the cubes had been easy to pack and there was plenty of space in their quarters for the children to explore safely.

Martha tightened her hold on her little boy. 'No. It's alright. I would rather keep him with me.'

Kira stared at her friend for a moment and then turned her attention to Kolwowsky, feeling a little hurt. 'How many people, families, do you have here?'

'Er... I'm not sure exactly. The internal monitors will give you access to the databank. I think we have about five hundred people here now. We had a new group arrive yesterday, just before you.'

'A new group? From where?' asked Jed.

'We have people coming from all over.' Kolwowsky helped himself to some more stew. 'Cities are becoming unstable all the time and resources are so tightly controlled by New Corp that most of 'em would've starved if they'd stayed where they were.' He seemed completely oblivious to the group's reaction to his words.

'How many cities have you contacted?' Jed was keen to find out exactly how widespread the Resistance was.

'I don't know. It's not my remit. Colonel Archer oversees that side of things. I'm sure she'd be happy to answer any questions you might have though.' Kolwowsky grinned at Jed before stuffing the last of his bread in his mouth.

Jed nodded and turned to speak to Ash in a low voice. 'I'm going to see what I can find out, keep your eyes and ears open as you check out Stores. We need to get a measure of Resistance.'

Ash nodded. They all had questions but the first thing they needed to do was gather as much information as possible.

The doors to the mess hall banged open and an incredibly drunk Russian staggered in, singing at the top of his voice, a bottle clutched tightly in one hand.

'Jed!' hissed Kira. 'Go get him before he causes any more disturbance!' She held an arm out for Peter and managed to balance both children on her knees.

Pushing his chair back, Jed stood and walked over to Artem, who had thankfully stopped singing and was looking around blearily.

'Jed! My comrade! Here, toast me.' Artem shoved the bottle in Jed's face while throwing a heavy arm around the man's shoulders.

Staggering slightly, Jed managed to turn the larger man towards the table where the others were sitting. Ignoring the stares from the rest of the room, he guided Artem over and half-dropped him onto the bench.

'Comrades!' bellowed Artem, looking blearily at them. 'Come! Drink with me.' He snagged the bottle back from Jed, sloshing the contents on the table before pouring large shots in several of the cups on the table. 'For lost ones!' he roared then downed a large shot.

Kira picked her shot up. 'For my parents,' she said before swallowing the liquor with a grimace.

'To Ruth,' said Dina in a small voice while Max echoed her and they both sank their shots.

'For the lost ones.' Ash held on to his dog tags as he drank, toasting his team who had all perished at the compound explosion.

'For the lost ones,' repeated Jed, watching his wife in concern as she tried to hold it together. Putting his cup down, he cleared his throat. 'I'll take him back to our rooms, then go find Archer. Everyone happy?'

There was murmured assent from the group as they prepared to leave the mess hall.

'Come on, big fella. Let's get you back to our rooms.' Jed heaved Artem up to his feet and let the drunk man lean heavily on him. 'Can you manage both?' he asked Kira.

She nodded and hefted the children onto her hips. Luckily it wasn't far to their quarters and the children were more interested in clinging on to Kira than getting down and exploring.

A swipe of his arm opened the doors and Jed staggered through to the communal area, dumping Artem on one of the sofas. At once, the large Russian began snoring gently.

'At least he looks peaceful,' Jed commented to Kira.

She shrugged slightly and put the children in the play cube. Keeping the volume low, she activated the play screen and left them watching educational cartoons. 'What do I do with him if he wakes up?'

'Try and get him into that room at the end. It's where we put his stuff.' Jed regarded the slumbering man. 'Perhaps several cups of synth-caf?'

Kira nodded and leaned into him for a quick hug. 'Be safe?'

'Always. Ping me on my wristplant if anything happens. I'll be as quick as I can. Will you be alright?'

'Yeah. I just need some rest. I'll be fine.' She smiled up at him. 'Go on, see what you can find out from Archer.' She looked over at the internal screen. 'If I get chance, I'll look on their system and see what's on there.'

Jed kissed her on the forehead, said goodbye to the children and left.

Kira looked at the sleeping man and the entertained children and decided to make herself a drink. In the kitchen area, she turned to say something to her mum, then gasped as the full force of her grief hit. Her vision swam and she bit her fist, trying to stop the tears. A low cry escaped her involuntarily and she doubled over. She couldn't stop the tears from coming or the loud sobs from escaping. Kira flinched as thick arms encircled her.

'I am sorry. I am so, so sorry.' It was Artem; he'd left the couch without her noticing and was holding her gently. 'Cry for them. For your mother, your father. For Ruth and little girl. For all innocents caught in fire.' He was talking in a low voice, a continual stream of comforting phrases as he held her in her grief.

Kira cried and cried and cried until she thought she

didn't have any tears left. It was almost silent. Tears flooded down her face as she took large gulping breaths, unable to halt the sobs, completely oblivious to everything around her. As her crying subsided, Kira remembered where she was.

'Are the children alright?' She tried to move, to see into the cube but Artem was holding onto her more tightly than she realised. Paying more attention to the man holding her, she realised his shoulders were still shaking. Her grief had unlocked his own, now it was her turn to clumsily hold him.

'It's alright, it wasn't your fault. You couldn't have known what would happen, none of us could.' She tried to comfort him as he'd comforted her and together, they stayed slumped on the kitchen floor until both had finished weeping.

Chapter Five

Dina and Ash followed Kolwowsky down a corridor, not really listening to him as he kept up a running commentary of where they were in the base.

'You alright?' asked Ash quietly.

Dina glanced sidewise at Ash. 'Yeah, you?'

'Not really.' He looked up at Kolwowsky to make sure he wasn't paying them any attention. 'I can't believe what happened. I can't believe we lost so many people at once.'

'I know. First, they wiped out City 15 and then... and then Artem's place. Part of me feels relieved that we got away but then I feel guilty for even thinking that. Like I shouldn't be glad I'm alive when all those people are dead.' Dina blinked hard and cleared her throat. 'And you and Jed, you lost your team, every operative. How do you deal with that?'

Ash glanced at Kolwowsky again, he was still talking. Something about solar panels and renewable energy supplies. 'To be honest, I don't know. They were my friends, people I worked with, people I respected. It's like they're on another mission or something. Like they're not really gone. But I think... I think Jed is having a tougher time with it.'

'Because of Kira's parents?'

'Not just because of them. Did you see how he reacted in the plane? He went into some kind of shock. I think he was reliving the attack on Corp Tech. I heard him whisper Ingrid's name.' Ash looked at Dina to see what she thought.

'I can understand why the destruction of Artem's place would trigger those memories for him. I guess we keep an eye on him, look out for any signs that he's struggling to deal with things. I keep thinking Ruth and Sarah must have survived somehow.' She paused and stopped walking. 'Because... because, how could they? How could New Corp kill a baby?' With a hand to her mouth she started crying.

Kolwowsky stopped walking and turned back in surprise. Ash shook his head at the soldier who made to walk towards Dina and put his own arm around her. From one of his pockets he found a tissue and offered it to her.

'We have to believe they are in a better place now. Hold on to the thought that Sarah is with Ruth, that they are together.' Ash didn't know whether his words were comforting or not. It was how he tried to think about it. Not that Ruth and Sarah had been brutally murdered but that they were together, somewhere else. It seemed to work as Dina stopped crying and took some gulping breaths to try and steady herself.

'Are you okay?' Kolwowsky was concerned. 'Can I take you to medical or something?'

'No, no, I'm okay. It's just... been a tough day.' Dina sniffed and wiped her nose on the rapidly disintegrating tissue before shoving in her pocket. 'Come on, let's carry on.'

'Ah, we're here.' Kolwowsky waved his arm at the

nearest door and it swung open to reveal the Stores area and a large screen in front of metal shelving that reached backwards into the warehouse, disappearing into the gloom. There was a pattern on the screen that swirled and pulsed. A pleasant male voice issued from speakers on the side.

Hello, Lieutenant Kolwowsky. It is good to see you. You have seventeen credits left on your account. What would you like to order today?

'Hello, Frank. I don't want to order anything today, thank you.' Kolwowsky grinned at the others. 'May I introduce you to two new members of Resistance. This is Dina and Ash. You should have them on your personnel list. Please confirm.'

The pattern on the screen changed and shifted its focus over to where Dina and Ash were standing.

'Fascinating,' breathed Ash.

Hello, Mr Ash. Hello, Miss Grey. Welcome to the Resistance. You each have fifty credits on your account. What would you like to order today?

'Er...' Dina's mind went blank. What did they need to order?

'Bring up a supplies list please, Frank.' Kolwowsky came to the rescue. The screen changed from its swirly pattern to a list of things available and Kolwowsky explained. 'It's an interactive screen, touch the area that you're interested in and Frank will list everything he has under that subheading. Look.' And he tapped the heading Personal Hygiene. A list of available items appeared including shampoo, toothbrushes and soap.

'Oh, okay, I see.' Dina moved forward eagerly. 'Let's see, we need some baby milk and some more synth-caf, probably some toothpaste and oh look, biscuits. Let's have some of those.' She continued to murmur to herself as she found her way round the system. 'Okay, I think I'm done. Do you want to add anything, Ash?'

He chuckled as he shook his head.

I'm sorry. You have insufficient credits for this order. Please review what you have selected.

Dina's face fell.

'Don't worry. We can sort that out,' Kolwowsky said. He turned to the screen. 'Frank? Please add Operative Ash and Miss Grey's allowance together.'

Confirmed. I'm sorry. You have insufficient credits for this order. Please review what you have selected.

'Uh... Frank? Please add Martha Hamble's allowance to the order?' asked Dina.

I am unable to comply. Individuals must be present in order for their credits to be used. I'm sorry. You have insufficient credits for this order. Please review what you have selected.

'How much are they short please, Frank?' Kolwowsky wanted Ash and Dina to take away everything they'd ordered.

This order requires an additional three credits.

Kolwowsky breathed a sigh of relief. 'Please take three credits from my allowance to complete this order.'

'No, we couldn't!' exclaimed Dina but he waved his hand at her.

'Don't worry, I get a refreshed credit allowance tomorrow. Besides, you need this stuff, biscuits and all.'

Thank you. Your order is complete. Please wait.

There was a whirring sound.

'That's the automated pickers. They will go and get the things off the shelf for you and bring the items here for you to collect. It won't take long.' There was a pause as they waited for the automatons to finish. A receipt churned out from the bottom of Frank's screen.

Kolwowsky picked it up and scanned it. 'Ah. That's where all your credits went. On the baby milk.' He pointed it out as he passed the receipt over to Dina.

'Why is that so expensive?' she asked.

'I guess because your babies are the only ones we have here, and it must be in short supply. The less we have of something, the more credits it costs. It's Frank's way of trying to stop us being wasteful with our resources. It's not easy to replace some of this stuff.'

'Will we be able to get more? I don't think the younger children are old enough to move onto solids yet,' asked Dina.

'Frank will alert Colonel Archer if an item low in stock is being regularly requested and then we see whether we can produce more in-house or...' He trailed off, not sure whether he should continue.

'Or?' prompted Ash.

'Or whether we can get it from outside. But that's really not my remit. Ah, your order.' Relieved that the conversation was interrupted, Kolwowsky opened the hatch and let the items be pushed through by one of the pickers. There were a couple of hover baskets on the ground and he started to fill one up with their items. 'You can use one of these to take your things back to your rooms. Bring it back when you're done. We don't have that many and everyone needs to use Stores.'

Dina and Ash nodded and watched how he activated the basket.

'Pretty neat bit of tech,' commented Ash. 'Is it an in-house build?'

'Yeah, we have a great tech department. If you have the necessary clearance, I can take you over there. They're always looking for new recruits, their gadgets are in high demand.'

'I can imagine,' murmured Dina.

'How do we know what level clearance we have?' asked Ash.

'Oh, right. If you go to your internal screen in your rooms and wave your wrist at the scanner on the bottom, it will load up your clearance, how many credits you have left, your work assignment, that sort of thing.'

'Work assignment?'

'Yeah, we all pitch in around here. The Resistance needs everyone to pull together and everyone to contribute.' Kolwowsky grinned at them before ushering them out of Stores and together with their laden hover basket they walked back to their quarters.

Chapter Six

'Left out of here and down to the end,' commented Max as he held the mess hall door open for Martha. 'Do you want me to carry something?' He looked on as Martha struggled to hoist her son back onto her hip and prevent her bag from falling off her opposite shoulder.

'No, I can manage.'

The bag fell off her shoulder, and as it landed on the floor the clasp undid and things rolled out. Among them the little blue Gaia statue and a holocube picture of Ruth, Martha, Lucas and Sarah. In her haste to snatch the cube up, Martha staggered and nearly fell, half dropping Lucas to the floor. He began crying in surprise at being nearly dropped.

'For frag's sake!' shouted Martha and she dropped to her knees letting go of her son but grabbing the holocube. She put her head in her hands to hide her face.

'Hey, it's alright. It's just a bag.' Max bent down to pick up the various items on the floor and put them back. Then he picked up Lucas, slung the bag over his shoulder and held a hand out to Martha. 'Come on. Let's go get some air.'

She looked up at him, her hair hanging across her face, and considered refusing his helping hand, but realised she was being petulant, so she grabbed it and pulled herself up off the floor. Clutching the holocube tightly she looked at her son.

'I can carry him to the allotment. He's not heavy,' Max offered.

Martha nodded. She desperately wanted to snatch her son back, to keep him safe, to prevent anything bad from happening to him, but she knew she was being irrational. Nothing would happen to Lucas while he was being carried by Max. She looked down at the holocube in her hand and squeezed her eyes shut. Even looking at a picture of her friend was too much. She reached over and tucked the holocube into the side pocket of the bag Max was carrying.

Max started walking slowly down the corridor and Martha soon followed. They didn't speak and she was grateful for the silence. She knew she was experiencing shock at losing her friend and Kira's parents. About fleeing her country and being here at the camp of Resistance. She had a hundred questions for Zac, a thousand really but all she really wanted to do was curl up with her son somewhere safe and warm, miles away from anyone who would try to hurt them.

As they neared the end of the corridor, Martha noticed a set of double doors that led outside the compound.

'This must be it,' she said as she waved her arm in front of the doors to open them. Nothing happened for a moment then the doors swung open ponderously.

Nature assaulted their senses. Martha could smell soil and herbal fragrances with the sour tang of manure underlying everything. Everywhere she looked there were splashes of green and the faintest buzz of insects in the air. She moved forward eagerly to see for herself what the Resistance was growing in their allotments.

'Here, this needs to be spread over bed four.' A short woman pointed to the far corner where a new raised bed was being prepared and tossed a bag of compost at Martha who barely caught it. 'You can press these seeds into bed three. That's half a dozen every half an inch.' She slapped a packet of seeds in Max's spare hand and didn't seem to notice the baby boy clinging to his other side. 'When you've finished, come and see me in greenhouse five. We have a replanting disaster to deal with.' When neither of them moved, the woman clapped her hands loudly. 'Chop, chop! We have lots to do.' She marched away from them, in the apparent direction of the greenhouses.

Max looked to Martha, but she had already started walking over to bed four, intent on carrying out her instructions. He dithered for a moment, but Lucas wasn't that heavy, and he could easily put a couple of seeds into some soil. He found that kneeling worked best as he shuffled along the side of the planter, but after a short while, his arm holding Lucas was burning with the continuous dead weight of the small child. Max craned his neck to look at the boy's face and realised he was asleep. Spying an empty wheelbarrow nearby and some flat hessian sacks, Max made a little nest for the boy and placed the sleeping child inside. He waited a moment to make sure Lucas didn't wake up then bent back to his seeding task.

Martha was tilling the compost gently into the bed. It felt good to feel the soil beneath her fingers, reconnecting herself with nature. She felt the ball of stress inside her ease slightly and started to breathe more regularly. She shied away from any thoughts of Ruth or Sarah, instead focusing intently on the task before her.

When she had finished, she turned to see Max had also finished but there was no sign of Lucas.

'What have you done with my son?' Martha shrieked, flying towards Max, clawed hands aiming for his face.

Max deftly caught her wrists and shushed her, tilting his head to the wheelbarrow at the side of him. Martha slumped in his hold and took a shaky breath, dispelling the panic that had threatened to overcome her.

'I am sorry. I just... I panicked when I couldn't see him.' She looked down at the sleeping boy in the wheelbarrow, clenching her hands to stop them from shaking. 'That is an ingenious use for one of those.'

'Is it okay?'

'Yes, he's fine.' Martha looked over towards the greenhouses. 'Shall we?'

Max nodded and began wheeling. Martha started picking the dirt out of her nails as she looked around her at the variety of plants growing. Looking up she couldn't see the tell-tale shimmer of a dome.

'I thought the entire base here was under a dome?'

'That's what they said.'

Martha pointed upwards and Max took in the lack of shimmer.

'Huh,' he said. He looked around. 'Maybe we're at the back end of the base and the dome doesn't stretch that far?'

'It's not exactly secure though, is it?'

They arrived at the greenhouse and Max gently manoeuvred the wheelbarrow inside. It was steamy and smelled loamy. The short woman they'd seen earlier was to their left muttering under her breath as she examined the tomato plants currently sitting in rows.

'Ah, you're here. Right, we have to get these tomatoes replanted into richer soil to increase their yield.

The new pots are over there.' She pointed to the bench opposite the tomato plants. 'Come on, no time to waste.'

Max parked the wheelbarrow and started at one end of the bench, while Martha took the middle. The woman finally took a proper look at them.

'You're not my gardeners. Where are you from? Have you been decontaminated?' She peered at them suspiciously.

'We are from, er... we are new, recently arrived and no, we have not been decontaminated. I did not know we were supposed to have been.' Martha had stopped what she was doing, mindful of the delicate plants in front of her.

The woman sniffed. 'You should be alright. Don't stop now, these plants need to be rehomed.' She glared at them for a few moments as they continued repotting. 'Who are you then, anyway?'

Forgetting where he was, Max launched into an introduction. 'I'm Dr Max Carter, I headed up a research station called Camp Eden just outside of City 42. We were investigating how the planet has been recovering from The Event and testing out new strains of edible plants, ones that were more disease resistance, quicker growers, that sort of thing.'

A gleam of interest lit up the woman's eyes. 'Did you bring samples with you? Seeds or seedlings?'

'I... uh... no. Sorry. We left in a bit of a hurry. But I did bring my research files, I'd be happy to share our findings with you.'

'That's something, I suppose. Shame you didn't have better priorities. We could've used a fresh injection of viable plants.' The woman continued working for a few moments before addressing Martha. 'And you, who are you? Another scientist from this camp?'

'No, I am a botanist, or was a botanist. My name is Martha Hamble.'

'Is it now? You're a disgraced governor who lost control of her city, way I heard it. No mention of being a botanist.' She noticed Martha stiffen at her remark. 'Yes, we get the sweeps over here, sometimes. We know what's happening on that little island of yours.' She looked at the row of plants Martha had re-potted. 'But you seem to know what you're doing I'll give you that. There's a place for you, for both of you, here. If you want it. If you haven't had your work assignments yet.'

Max shook his head. 'No, we haven't had those yet.'

'You will. Everyone in the Resistance is assigned somewhere. I'll put a request in, if you like. Colonel Archer knows I need more hands down here.'

'That is very kind,' replied Martha. 'But who exactly are you?'

'I'm Bennett, Lisa Bennett. Head grower and hardest worker in the Resistance.' She caught Max smiling at her statement. 'Oh, you think someone else works harder than me? Plants don't grow themselves you know.' And Bennett stomped off, calling behind her. 'And take your kid out of my wheelbarrow!'

Martha retrieved him swiftly and motioned for Max to follow her out of the greenhouse.

'What an odd woman,' remarked Martha.

'I kinda liked her. I'd be happy to work here, if we do get assigned.'

'I suppose we'll have to wait and see. We'd better get back to the others, let them know what we've found.' Martha kept hold of Lucas this time but seemed happy for Max to carry her bag. Working in the gardens had relaxed her a little and she was intrigued to learn more about Bennett and her allotment.

Chapter Seven

Jed walked confidently down the corridor but in fact he had no idea where he was going. He was hoping he'd come across Archer or Kolwowsky but so far, he had yet to see anyone. After reaching a second dead end, he leant on the wall and sighed heavily.

Voice activation accepted. Hello, Captain Jenkins, how may I assist you?

Jed flinched at the unexpected voice and noticed the flat panel on the wall beside him.

'And who are you?'

My name is Lola. How may I assist you?

'Er... I'm looking for Colonel Archer.'

Colonel Archer is currently in her office. May I direct you?

'Yes, please, Lola.'

Follow the blue line and you will soon reach your destination. Have a pleasant day, Captain Jenkins.

'Er... you too, Lola.' Jed felt a little silly talking to the wall but was impressed at the blue arrows that appeared along the corridor, highlighting the direction he needed to walk in order to find Colonel Archer. Now that he had some guidance, it didn't take him long to get to where he wanted to be.

Waving his arm at the entrance where the arrows ended, Jed expected to be able to go through straight away, but the doors did not open. Nothing happened. He could hear voices talking, so he rapped smartly and waited. The voices stopped talking and the doors slid open as Colonel Archer stood in the doorway.

She blinked in surprise. 'Jenkins. Can I help you?'

Jed pushed past her and was satisfied to see Zac was also in the room.

'Yes. You can start by answering my questions,' he said.

Archer exchanged a glance with Zac before gesturing to the table and chairs on the far side of the room. 'Maybe we should sit down.'

'I'm fine, thanks,' replied Jed stiffly and watched them both take a seat before continuing. 'Look, Zac, you led us to believe you were a museum owner's son, biding his time in City 9. Then Artem's complex gets destroyed, my entire team is massacred, and you fly us over here where for some insane reason you are apparently in charge of the whole fragging Resistance. You owe me an explanation.' Jed was breathing hard by the time he'd finished talking. It had taken all his self-control not to grab hold of Zac and physically shake him.

'How dare you speak to the General like that! If it wasn't for him, you and your family would never have made it here.' Archer leapt to Zac's defence.

'Archer, it's fine.' Zac waved a hand at his second-in-command. 'You're right, Jed. You do deserve an explanation. Please, sit down.'

Jed scowled at Zac but took a seat. He leant back and crossed his arms, waiting for the excuses to begin.

'Firstly, my aunt and uncle did own that museum but yes, I was using it as a cover for my work with the

Resistance.' He paused and smiled briefly at Archer. 'I have only recently been promoted to General.'

'Okay, well...' Jed was thrown, he hadn't expected Zac to start explaining things straight away. 'Look, I can understand not coming right out and telling us you were Resistance, that's common sense. But what about my team, my in-laws, Ruth and...' Jed trailed off.

'I had no idea New Corp would make a move like that. If I had had the slightest clue, I would have made sure everyone left the complex, together. I honestly thought your team, and everyone else, would be perfectly safe. Artem was planning on flying straight back to continue our intelligence monitoring. Obviously, that is no longer the case.'

'So now you're flying blind.'

'Not entirely but yes, we don't have the same information coverage we did have. But New Corp are predictable; free thinkers are not exactly encouraged,' replied Zac.

Archer coughed gently and flicked her glaze to the open handheld on Zac's desk.

'We are in the middle of planning a memorial service. For the people you lost. We want to show you that the Resistance is deeply sorry you were targeted. We lost some people at Artem's place too.' A shadow fell across Zac's face.

'I appreciate that, we all will. It's important to say goodbye, even when there's nothing to say goodbye to.' Jed pushed away the memory of his sister, keeping his emotions in check. He changed subject brusquely. 'Where did you get all your tech from? Kolwowsky was talking about an AI in Stores, I met Lola on my way here - how is that the case?'

This time Archer replied. 'It's true we are the

Resistance but we're also all that's left. We have the best minds here and have scavenged much of our material from abandoned cities.'

Jed interrupted. 'What do you mean, you're all that's left. All that's left of what?'

'The human race. There are small settlements in zones one and two, we're all that's left of zone three and we haven't been able to make contact with zone four.'

Jed burst out laughing, waiting for Zac and Archer to stop their charade and join in. When he realised they weren't, his laughter died.

'Are you serious?'

Zac nodded and went to the info screen. He tapped a few buttons and pulled up an old map of the world, but Jed wouldn't let him continue.

'Stop. Stop. If this is going to be some grand explanation, I want the rest of my family here with me. This is life-changing information. I don't want to explain it third hand.'

'Of course, I agree. You should all be briefed fully.' Zac glanced at his wristplant. 'Let's meet back here, tomorrow, after breakfast. Say 9am - is that alright?'

Jed nodded and stood to leave but before he left the room, he hesitated.

'Are we really all that's left?'

Zac nodded and Archer said yes softly. Jed's eyes flicked to the map on the wall again, but it didn't mean anything to him. He wasn't even sure where they were on that thing.

'I'll see you tomorrow,' he said and left the room.

'That went well,' remarked Archer. 'Are you sure about telling them everything? It might not be wise yet, we don't even know whether they're going to stay.'

'I think it's a bit late for that, Archer. We need them

on our side if we have any chance of pulling this off.'

Jed heard what they said, he was loitering in case it had all been a joke at his expense. It hadn't. He waved at an info panel on the wall. Lilac colours swirled in response.

Good evening, Captain Jenkins. How may I assist you?

'Take me to my quarters please, Lola.'

Of course. Please follow the green line. Have a pleasant evening.

A green line appeared on the wall and Jed followed it down the corridor, his fingertips touching the wall lightly, his thoughts whirling.

Chapter Eight

Dina and Ash were the first back to their quarters. A very quiet Kira met them while Artem slept off his vodka in his bunk. They could hear his snores rumbling in the background.

'Here, let me help,' Kira said in a low voice as she helped Dina to unload the hover basket and put the food away. 'I don't want to wake Artem or the kids.'

Kira grinned when she picked up the chocolate biscuits and hugged Dina at discovering the baby milk.

'It should help for a bit, right?' Dina wasn't sure she'd brought the right thing.

'It's great, thank you.' Kira nudged the empty hover basket with her foot. 'What do we do with this?'

'I'll take it back to Stores. I don't think we're meant to keep them,' offered Ash and he left them brewing synth-caf. He was hurrying back to make sure he got a look in at the chocolate biscuits when he bumped into Jed on the way.

'Alright, Ash? How did it go at Stores?' asked Jed.

'We were able to order some supplies, but we had to think on our feet, hopefully we haven't missed anything, Sir.'

Jed sighed. 'I think rank is moot when there's only

two of us left, Ash. Call me Jed,' and he held out his hand to his remaining operative.

Ash shook the proffered hand firmly and grinned. 'You know, Sir, er... I mean Jed, my name is actually Matthew.'

'Really?'

'Yes, Sir. I mean, Jed.'

Both men laughed.

'I guess we've both got to get used to this,' said Jed as he waved his arm over the door plate at their quarters. Walking in, he saw that everyone was back from their explorations.

'I know you've probably all got something to tell the rest of us, but I'd like to get the children in bed before we lose track of time,' Kira said without her usual enthusiasm.

Jed shot her a concerned look but picked Peter up and followed his wife into their chosen bedroom.

'Are you okay?' he asked as he wrestled Peter out of his day clothes.

'I'm fine,' replied Kira and she tossed him a night-time nappy for the little boy.

Before Jed could press his wife further, they were joined by Martha and Lucas, who was giggling away as his mum tickled him. Martha dropped three bottles of milk gently onto the bed.

'I made these up for them. You are not planning on coming back out again with them, are you?' she asked.

'No, it's bedtime,' replied Kira as she grabbed one of the bottles and sat on the bed with Grace.

Martha and Jed followed with Lucas and Peter and soon the three children were drifting off into contented sleep.

'Shall we put them all down together for now?' asked

Martha. 'I can always move Lucas into my room later. I think he finds it comforting to sleep with the others.' She looked down fondly at the slumbering child.

'Yeah, that's fine,' replied Kira and she tapped the sleeping cube to expand it enough to fit all three children.

They joined the others in the communal area. Artem had reappeared, a little bleary eyed but visibly perking up with a strong cup of synth-caf in front of him.

'Is good to be with you,' he said simply.

The others murmured their agreement.

'Dina, Ash, what did you find out?' asked Jed, taking charge.

'Stores is indeed run by an AI called Frank. The computer system assigns credits and keeps track of what you spend. We can pool our credits to buy more things but only with the people there in the room at the time of order,' Ash explained.

'The more expensive items are the ones in short supply, things like the baby milk unfortunately,' added Dina.

'Although Kolwowsky did say that if a short supply item becomes popular then they try to make more or source more from trips outside the dome. But I get the feeling those are few and far between,' finished Ash.

'Is true. Great lab here, great workshop. You want, they make. They can't make, maybe you find but, is hard.' Artem concurred.

'Okay, let's hope they can make more formula for us.' Jed turned to Martha and Max. 'What about you, did you find the allotment?'

'Yes. We met with the head gardener, Bennett. It was... useful,' replied Martha.

'Useful? What does that mean?' asked Dina.

'We helped plant some seeds and repot some tomatoes.'

'So, you didn't actually find out anything then.' Jed looked disappointed.

Martha glared at Jed but before she had chance to say anything, Max stepped in.

'That's a little unfair, Jed. We found the allotments, we got our hands dirty, we saw the breadth of seedlings and what plants they are growing. I also agreed to share my research from Camp Eden with Bennett to help them with crop yield and disease resistance. But I tell you one thing, they are not growing that much produce. Possibly enough for a couple of hundred people. Depending on whether there was much more that we didn't see.'

Jed held his hands up in apology and paused to make sure Martha had nothing else to add.

'Right, I went to find Zac. And Archer,' he said.

'What did you say?' asked Martha.

'I challenged him. I wanted to know why the hell he lied to us back in City 9 and whether he had any prior knowledge of the attack on Artem's compound.'

'Zac would not do this. If he knew, all would be saved. Zac is good man,' rumbled Artem.

'That's what he said. He claims to have no idea about the attack and he... they are planning to hold a memorial service for everyone that died.' Jed paused to look at his wife, but her face was expressionless. 'He said they lost people too.' When no one said anything, he pressed on. 'I asked about all the tech here and he said... well, he basically said that the Resistance did the best with what's left.'

'What do you mean, what's left? What's left of what?' asked Martha.

'Of us. Of the human race. He started talking about

zones and settlements, but my mind was reeling. I told him I wanted him to tell all of us together and explain it properly.'

'That's ridiculous!' interrupted Dina. 'There has to be more people out there. I don't believe you.'

'He wants to see us all after breakfast tomorrow so he can explain everything.'

'He has a lot of fragging explaining to do,' muttered Martha and she was the first to stand and say goodnight. She ducked into Kira and Jed's room to collect Lucas and called a quiet goodnight to the others.

Kira also said goodnight and went to check on Grace and Peter while Dina pulled Max along with her into their room.

'Come, Ash, you bunk with me. I'll tell you a bedtime story.' Artem chuckled as he clapped an arm on Ash's shoulder and guided him to their shared room, leaving Jed to follow his wife and try and get some rest.

'Are you sure you're alright?' whispered Jed as he tried to get undressed quietly.

'No, not really, but there's nothing anyone can do.'

'I'm here for you, you know that, right? Anything I can do, just ask.' Jed felt helpless. Kira had been a rock when he was working through his grief for Pete and Ingrid but now, she was shutting him out and he didn't know how to help her.

Kira gave him a quick peck on the cheek as he got into bed then turned away from him, wrapped up in her corner of the duvet. Jed knew that meant *leave me alone* and so he stared at the ceiling, trying to will himself to sleep.

Chapter Nine

'Thank you all for coming,' Zac said as he addressed the group of people in front of him.

Jed was pissed off. Zac had led him to believe that he would be explaining everything to him and his friends but there were other small groups of strangers in the briefing room. Each group remained clumped together with the people they had arrived with; no-one had ventured anything apart from the odd awkward smile between strangers.

'I think these must be the other new arrivals,' whispered Dina to the others.

'What makes you think that?' asked Jed, peevishly.

'Kolwowsky mentioned there had been another group of refugees arrive yesterday.'

'He did?' Ash sounded surprised.

'Yeah, you should have been listening instead of drooling over Frank,' teased Dina with a goodhearted grin.

Ash chuckled quietly but was hushed by Jed as Zac continued speaking.

'I'd like to take this opportunity to formally welcome you to the Resistance.' He swept a glance across the room. 'Sounds scary, doesn't it? The Resistance. I'm sure some of you must be wondering, resistance to what exactly? Well, we resist against the corrupt organisation of New Corp, previously known as Corporation, who are more interested in profit and power then they are working with the planet to save what's left.' He tapped the large info board behind him, and an old-fashioned map of the planet appeared. 'This is what Earth used to look like. Seven continents, thousands of cities, billions of people.' He tapped again. 'This is what Earth looks like today.'

Everyone leaned forward to get a good look.

'As you can see, what was North America was badly affected by the radiation of The Event. There are also large tracts of scorched earth in much of what used to be Asia and central Europe.' He pointed to large yellow areas on the map. 'As far as we have been able to determine these areas have not yet recovered. The small green patches are renewed earth.' There weren't many green patches. 'When Corporation set up the initial fifty cities, they renamed the continents into zones, Zone 1 is South America, Zone 2 is southern Africa, Zone 3 is what's left of Europe and Asia and Zone 4 is Oceania.'

'What about the blue lines around all the land masses? And the sections coloured in blue. What do they represent?' It was someone from one of the other groups asking.

'That indicates the amount of land we have already lost or will eventually lose if the ocean continues to rise at its current rate.'

There was a sobering silence. All of North America was submerged in blue apart from a small section of uninhabitable yellow. South America had lost its southern tip, Africa its northern half. A thick blue line ran all around Europe and what wasn't yellow in Russia,

India and China was blue. Nearly all of Australia was marked out blue as well.

'Where are we on that map, exactly?' asked Jed.

'We're here.' Zac pointed to a section of mostly blue. 'Formerly Scandinavia, currently the Resistance stronghold but as you can see, not for much longer.'

'Do you think the oceans are still rising then?' asked Dina.

'We believe that we are at the beginning of a mass extinction event. The polar ice caps have lost their war with rising global temperatures, thanks to the after-effects of The Event, and all that meltwater will raise the current levels significantly. Plus, additional displacement thanks to post-glacial rebound.'

'But that means most of our country will be flooded!' exclaimed Dina.

Zac nodded grimly. 'As well as large parts of the rest of the world. We cannot ignore the science; we must head to higher ground. Specifically, here.' He tapped a large white area in the middle of Zone 3. 'These are the Ural Mountains, the border between the former East Europe and West Siberia. Historically this area has been populated by nomadic tribes who traditionally fished and hunted to survive, looked after the wild herds of reindeer and horses and some settlements that grew crops, we know we will be able to support ourselves here.'

'What about the other cities?' asked Jed.

'We are all that is left here in Zone 3.'

Dina barked a laugh. 'You cannot be serious?'

Colonel Archer spoke up. 'General Ridgley is nothing but serious. The people we have managed to collect here are all that remain in this zone.'

'Except for New Corp citizens in City 9 and 42,' Martha remarked drily.

'But what about the other cities?' Jed asked again.

'We have received intel that there are two surviving settlements, one in zone one and one in zone two. As yet, we have been unable to make contact with zone four. The infrastructure does not currently exist for us to travel out to these zones and as you know, Corporation were restrictive on communication between cities.' Zac glanced at Archer before continuing. 'It is my hope that once we have relocated, teams will volunteer to travel out and make contact.'

Archer blinked; this was news to her.

'This is what we know so far.' Zac tapped the info screen again and brought up a list of cities. There was silence as the room digested the information.

Formerly Europe
City 1 – originally set up to be like Earth-that-was, decimated by plague. No inhabitants.
City 6 – approached by Resistance and agreed to join
Cities 9 & 42 – under New Corp control. Population unknown.
City 15 – destroyed by New Corp. No survivors.
City 20 – faulty power supply, New Corp refused aid. Reconnaissance team deployed, awaiting report.
City 36 –affected by radiation poisoning, there will be no survivors.
City 40 – flooded, survivors joined Resistance.

Formerly North Africa
Cities 2, 33, 39 & 45 – flooded, survivors believed to have joined the single settlement for survivors in Zone 2

Formerly Southern Africa
Cities 10, 14, 18, 24, 28 & 31 – believed to have joined

the single settlement for survivors in Zone 2

Formerly Asia
City 5 – a landslide knocked out the power and comms, New Corp denied requests for help. Survivors joined Resistance. No inhabitants.
Cities 7 & 46 – approached by Resistance and agreed to join
Cities 11, 26 & 37 – city succumbed to radiation sickness, no survivors
City 16, 22, 30 & 34 – flooded, believed to have fled to Zone 4
City 41 – New Corp withdrew food and medical supplies with reports of a suspected attack. Survivors joined Resistance. No inhabitants.
City 43 – reconnaissance team deployed, awaiting report.

Formerly Oceania
Cities 3, 12, 32 & 35 –unable to make contact. Survivors unknown.
Cities 19, 21, 27 & 48 believed to have been flooded.

Formerly North America
Cities 4 & 8 – flooded, survivors believed to have fled to Zone 1
Cities 44 & 49 – affected by radiation, no known survivors

Formerly South America
Cities 13, 17, 29 & 38 – believed to have joined the single settlement for survivors in Zone 1
Cities 23 & 25 – flooded, believed to have fled to Zone 1

City 50 – originally set up to be the pinnacle of Corporation life. Population and official allegiance unknown.

'How did you get hold of this information?' asked Jed.

'The refugees that have come here brought their stories and intel with them. New Corporation had varying success in consolidating its power depending on the greater distance they had to cover in order to control the city populations. We have been able to send out sorties to cities in the immediate vicinity of our base. Others were reported as empty by travellers on their way here. We've managed to hack some satellites and get real-time imagery for parts of the different zones. It's taken time but this is what we've been able to piece together.'

'Why did we not know about you before?' asked Martha.

'Your city was based on an island that happened to be a Corporation, and now New Corp, stronghold. We had no way of getting a message to you without compromising our own security. Until now.'

'But there are so many more people in City 42. People I know, people I have to help,' objected Martha.

'And we will do what we can but as you know, New Corp has demonstrated they have significant firepower and are clearly unafraid of using that destruction. I don't want to put lives at risk unnecessarily.'

'You're going to leave all those people to drown.' It was the first time Kira had spoken.

'We will do everything we can to help those we can help.'

'What about the cities that are in Australia and New Zealand? It says no information on your city list.' Max intervened with another question.

'We have been unable to raise any communications with Oceania. And it's impossible to travel that far with our limited fuel and transport resources. Travelling there by boat would take too long. The decision was made to establish a safe and secure base and then in the future we will be able to make contact with them.'

'Yeah, right,' muttered Kira.

'So, your plan is to move everyone from your fortified base here up some mountain somewhere and hope for the best?' asked Jed. He was uneasy at the thought of leaving what he'd figured to be a safe place.

'More or less, yes.' Zac gave a short laugh but no-one else joined in. He stopped and waited in the silence that followed for any more questions.

There were none.

'Look, I know this is a lot to process. All this information is available to you via your info screens in your quarters. Take a couple of days to process everything. Come and see me or Colonel Archer if you want anything clarifying and we'll do our best to answer your questions.' He turned to the Colonel and she stepped forward again.

'The memorial service for the men and women...'

'And child.' Kira's voice was loud as she interrupted Archer.

'...and child that we have lost recently will be held this afternoon in the Serenity Garden. Your individually assigned staff will come and collect you. Please don't stray from your quarters if you wish to attend.'

'We hope to see everyone at the service,' said Zac.

'Finally, because you are all new arrivals, your work orders will be sent through tomorrow,' Archer added.

'Work orders?' Jed queried.

She smiled thinly. 'Everyone in the Resistance contributes where they can, Jenkins. Everyone.'

Her tone suggested dismissal. The other groups of people started filing out the doors, but Kira stayed where she was. She walked up to Zac.

'You didn't say anything about Gaia.'

'I don't know anything about Gaia. You're the expert,' he replied.

'What exactly is it you're expecting her to do?'

'Nothing at all.'

Kira wrinkled her brow in confusion. 'But you said you wanted to be able to communicate with her.'

'We do. But I'm not hopeful. If the spirit of the Earth does exist and hasn't seen fit to do anything to save us by now, then I doubt she'll step in now. But...' Zac shrugged.

'You're covering all your bases. Trying to think smart.' Jed had joined the conversation.

'It's not like you can call her on the comm, you know. She'll only appear when she wants to,' Kira retorted.

'I know. But it's you, and your friends, that she has chosen to appear to. I hope if she does show her face, you'll share with the rest of us what she has to say.' Zac looked closely at Kira's face, to determine whether she would lie to him about it.

'If she speaks to me, I will tell you what she says.'

He nodded in satisfaction and said his goodbyes to the rest of them before leaving the room, Colonel Archer closely behind him.

'What the frag do we do now?' asked Dina but nobody had the answer.

Chapter Ten

'We go to our rooms like good little Resistance members and wait to be collected for the memorial.' Despite her scathing words, Kira's tone was leaden; there was no fire behind what she said. Leaving the others to do as they wished, she picked Grace up and carried her out of the briefing room. All the children had been as good as gold during the meeting, but Grace was starting to get fractious now. It was time for her milk.

The other followed dutifully. Even Artem was subdued and the mood didn't improve in their quarters. With everyone hanging around waiting to go to the service, tempers grew short, and after Ash had paced past Martha for the umpteenth time, she lost her cool.

'For frag's sake, Ash! Just sit down. Having you pacing up and down like that is getting on my nerves.'

Ash stopped instantly and plonked himself in the nearest seat. His knee began to jig, and Martha tutted loudly at him.

Dina looked at her wristplant again and sighed heavily.

'Instead of time watching, maybe you should think about what you want to say at the memorial,' suggested Kira quietly.

'Do you think they'll let us speak?' asked Dina.

Kira looked at her, eyes rimmed red. 'They won't stop me.'

Her quiet certainty calmed the others and brought them back to the fact that they had lost so many people. A different sort of stillness clung to them now as everyone reflected on their loss.

Finally, the door chimed and slid open. Kolwowsky stepped through, clad in a black jumpsuit this time, the colour choice a mark of respect.

'If you would all like to come with me?' He stood to one side to give them space to leave but Kira stayed in her chair, unable to move.

'What's wrong, hon?' Jed asked, going back for her.

'I don't want to say goodbye,' she replied in a small voice and buried her face in her husband's jumper.

Jed made soothing noises and gently lifted her to standing. With one arm wrapped round her, he led her through the door and out into the corridor. She could walk but she clung to him, head down, unwilling to look where they were going. Dina had Grace and Peter in the shared stroller while Martha had decided to carry Lucas. Since arriving at the Resistance, he had been extremely clingy.

Kolwowsky led them to an inner courtyard which was surrounded on all sides by the walls of the complex. Kira looked up to see blue skies and felt the sun's warmth on her skin. Something her parents would never know again. The thought was enough to make her catch her breath and she stumbled slightly, grabbing onto Jed for extra support. No-one seemed to notice and Kolwowsky gestured to one side where a row of seats stood empty. The group filed in and waited, feeling self-conscious for being at the front of the service.

Zac and Colonel Archer strode up onto a small raised dais, also dressed in black.

'They look smart,' whispered Dina to Max, who half smiled and put a finger to his lips.

'Thank you, everyone, for joining us on this sombre occasion. We are gathered here to honour our fallen. Let us start with a minute's silence.' Zac bowed his head and the other members of the Resistance in the room followed suit.

Jed looked as his friends and saw most of them had done the same. He ended up looking at his shoes but instead of thinking about the people he'd lost he felt a prickling on the back of his neck as if someone were staring right at him. Feeling self-conscious, he gradually lifted his head so as not to disturb anyone else and looked behind him. There was nothing there. Frowning, he went back to looking at the floor, but the prickling sensation didn't go away.

A gentle cough from Zac marked the end of the minute of silence.

'If anyone here would like to say something, please share your thoughts with the rest of us.' And he stepped back from the microphone. Initially no-one moved but then a tall, dark skinned woman with close-cropped hair walked up to the dais. Zac clasped hands with her and smiled encouragingly.

She bent forwards to talk into the microphone.

'My name is Finona. I come from City 20. We left because our power supply failed, and we lost many of our citizens. We walked many miles to come here. New Corporation denied us permission to leave our city and yet they also refused to accept us into City 9. We matter. I matter. And the friends and family that I lost matter. I remember them.' She was shaking slightly by the time she had finished.

Another person approached the dais. A young man of Indo-Asian descent. He was meticulously dressed in crisp white trousers and tunic. He bowed slightly to Zac before he approached the microphone.

'My name is Priya. I am from City 41. We did not leave from natural disaster. We left after New Corporation withdrew their food and medical supplies. My city was slowly starving to death. The journey here took the lives of many of my people. There are only a few of us left. But I will fight for their survival. Whatever it takes. I remember them.' Priya's eyes burned with zeal.

Kira made to walk up to the dais at the same time as Martha. They both stopped, then Martha took Kira's hand and they walked up together. Neither of them looked Zac in the eye.

'Hello, my name is Martha, and this is Kira. We came from City 42.' There was a soft gasp of recognition. 'We had overthrown the yoke of Corporation, but we were naive to think we had won. New Corporation are a more ruthless, power hungry entity than we could ever imagine and in our journey to get here we have lost friends, family, comrades and even an entire city. I remember them.' Martha finished and glanced at Kira to see if she still wanted to speak.

Kira stood closer to the microphone but took time to order her thoughts. Before she spoke, she grabbed Martha's hand and squeezed it tightly.

'I do not want to talk about regimes or fighting. I want to talk about my parents and friends whom I lost a few days ago. Jean and Malcolm Bishop were kind, loving and generous people who will always be missed, and not just by me.' While Kira's voice was steady, her grip on Martha's hand was like iron and tears were falling freely down her face. 'My friend, Ruth Maddocks and her baby girl, Sarah, who had barely begun to live, were both tragically lost in a senseless act of destruction for which I can never forgive. Ruth was the wild one, the rebellious streak in our group of friends, a true free spirit, and she will be missed so much.'

Artem blew his nose incredibly loudly, startling many of the listeners but making Kira smile slightly.

'We lost an entire team of operatives, soldiers if you will. Men and women who had pledged loyalty to Martha, and to my husband, Jed, and who had taken an oath to keep us safe. Instead it was them we should have kept safe.' She took a deep breath. 'I still feel like I will walk around the corner and see my family and friends. They are not lost to me and as long as I have breath in my body, I will honour their memory. Always.'

There wasn't a dry eye in the room when Kira and Martha stepped down, although Colonel Archer was doing her best to put her emotions back under control.

Zac stepped forward. 'If there is no-one else?' He waited but no-one was forthcoming, he continued with the memorial. 'In memory of the fallen we light a candle for them today and hold them forever in our hearts.'

Kolwowsky and the other Resistance soldiers handed out small candles to everyone in the room and brought lit tapers round to light them.

Kira felt a moment of peace as she stood in quiet contemplation with everyone else, staring at the flame in her hands. It didn't take away the aching loss she felt but it did make her feel like she'd be able to find the strength to carry on.

Chapter Eleven

The info wall chimed. Dina looked up.

'Hey, guys, looks like our work orders have come through. You'd better come and look at this,' she called to the others.

Everyone gathered around the monitor to read the allocations.

Martha Hamble - Allotment
Max Carter - Allotment
Dina Grey - Science & Technology
Matthew Ash - Science & Technology
Jed Jenkins - Peacekeeping
Artem Misner - Peacekeeping

'I didn't know your first name was Matthew!' exclaimed Dina staring at Ash in bemused embarrassment.

'It's fine, don't worry,' he replied, equally uncomfortable about the situation.

'Where is your allocation, Kira?' asked Martha but Kira shrugged. 'And what does *Peacekeeping* mean?'

'It's army. Or militia. Or playing with guns. Whatever you like to call it. Is good, da?' Artem thumped Jed on the shoulder, happy to be assigned with him.

Jed nodded. He was pleased to be in the action, but he was worried why Kira hadn't been assigned anywhere.

'I'm going to call Kolwowsky, see he knows anything about this,' he said, but Martha put a hand on his arm stopping him.

'Sorry, Jed, but I do not think there is any point in calling Kolwowsky.' She pointed at the screen. 'If you read the rest it says our assigned Resistance member will be here soon with our work permits and uniforms, he is already on his way.'

'Work permits? That sounds a bit...' Dina voice everyone's concerns.

'Look, let's see what Kolwowsky has to say. Working in the Resistance has to be a good thing, right? We can't sit here doing nothing. At least if we're working it will keep us busy, but it should also give us insight into how the Resistance works. Let's see if we can figure out what their overall goal is. Zac looks like a man with a plan to me.' Jed looked round the group to make sure everyone agreed with him. Artem was the only real loose cannon in the group but Jed felt his loyalty lay more with them than with Zac, because of what had happened to Ruth.

The door pinged then opened. It was Kolwowsky.

'Alright? I have all your uniforms and permits and everything. Let's get you all kitted out.' He was grinning widely, as usual, and gestured to the hover basket next to him.

'Why don't I have an assignment?' asked Kira.

'Uh… um... Colonel Archer thought you'd be too busy looking after the children and um...' Kolwowsky trailed off as everyone stared daggers at him. He raised his hands in submission. 'Hey, it's nothing to do with me. We don't have the facilities for babies here, there's a school but we can't put them in the classroom. Can we?'

'No, we cannot. Lucas will come with me to the allotment. I see no reason why I cannot work there with him by my side,' countered Martha.

'You'll have to take that up with Bennett yourself,' replied Kolwowsky doubtfully. He didn't think she would take too kindly to having children in her workspace.

'I will.'

'I don't mind looking after Grace and Peter,' said Kira quietly but no-one was listening to her.

'I'm going to give that Colonel Archer a piece of my mind. Who does she think she is assuming that Kira wants to look after children all day? Doesn't she know what a valuable team member she is?' Dina was livid, and Kolwowsly took a step back nervously.

'Look, I'm just telling you what she said...' he protested weakly.

'Well it's not good enough. I mean, honestly!' Dina fumed.

'Guys, I said I don't mind.' Kira tried again.

'It's one thing to tuck us all away down here, out of sight, out of mind, but if you think you are pushing my wife to the side lines, you can think again, Kolwowsky.' Jed took a step forward and was startled when his wife shouted.

'HEY! I said, I don't mind!' Once she had everyone's attention, Kira continued. 'I have no problems looking after Grace and Peter, Lucas too if you want me to, Martha. There's no need for an archivist here. We need to be looking to the future, not clinging to the past.'

'But all your knowledge... everything about the cities

and The Event... you are not thinking of letting all that go to waste?' protested Martha.

'Were you not there in that meeting? The cities are gone. The Event was over two hundred years ago. What we need to deal with today is the mass extinction disaster that threatens the lives of the people here and now. You don't need me to do that.'

Martha swallowed her retort, knowing that she would not win this argument with her friend. Instead, she gave Kira a quick hug and began talking to her about keeping Lucas for the day. She still thought she would be able to take him with her to Allotment on a regular workday but perhaps orientation wasn't the best place for him.

Jed frowned. His wife was right to a certain degree, but she was a fighter, and it wasn't like her to give in and give up. She should be burning with righteousness, not slumped in defeat. He decided he'd have to tackle it later. Now that he was in peacekeeping, he should be able to corner Archer and get an assignment sorted out.

'Okay, Kolwowsky. Give us the uniforms.' Jed held his hand out as the Lieutenant distributed the packages.

'Right, well. You've all got info jacks about your roles and where you need to report in. I'm on comms if you need me or have any questions. Good luck.' And he bid a hasty retreat.

'It's overalls,' said Martha, a little disappointed.

Max looked at his doubtfully. 'I'm not sure these will be long enough.'

'Maybe we can get a new pair exchanged over in Stores?' suggested Dina.

Max smiled at her and nodded towards her packaging. 'What have you got?'

She rummaged. 'Er... info jack, work permit, ooh, a

new handheld and a lab coat.' She sighed. 'It's so cliché.'

'It's also easy to spot and easy to make,' commented Ash who was secretly pleased with his assignment. He had expected to be turned into a soldier but was glad his tech expertise would be of some use.

'Yeah, alright, smart guy,' teased Dina while Max watched them both closely.

'Do you have an assignment, Artem?' asked Jed, looking in his kit bag. There was a note telling him to report to the training ground.

'Da. Training ground at 0900 tomorrow. They want to see how fit Artem is. Is ok. I show them muscles.' He smiled good-naturedly at Jed, but Jed had an uneasy feeling about what was going to happen next.

Chapter Twelve

Jed had been right to be apprehensive about his assignment to peacekeeping. He looked at the training field in dismay. New recruits. He was with all the new recruits and he hadn't even been asked to train them. He was one of them. Artem didn't seem fazed in the slightest. He was telling jokes with a couple of other Russians he'd managed to find. They were enjoying speaking in their mother tongue.

'Alright, ladies. Let's get down to business.' It was Colonel Archer.

Jed scowled at her as he waited to see what she had to say.

'You've been selected for peacekeeping because of your previous experience in your cities. Some of you have come from Force, some from Security. A few of you are ex-military from your old cities. Today, you forget all of that. Today, you are Resistance. Line up!'

People moved into a rough line but still clumped together in their known groups.

'On the line, at the double!' shouted Archer, pointing to a white line on the floor.

Everyone hurried to stand on it. Jed found himself midway, while Artem was off to the left.

'Welcome to your fitness test. Drop and give me twenty.'

Jed dropped and began doing press-ups, it was old school, but it was effective training. But not everyone seemed to know what they were supposed to do.

'Give you twenty what?' asked a young girl.

'Press-ups, recruit. Press-ups.' Archer gestured to those already on the ground, tapping her foot as she waited for everyone to comply.

Finished, Jed jumped up and stood ready, legs hip width apart, arms clasped behind him and waited to see what he'd be asked to do next. They were made to do sit ups, run suicides, more press-ups, more sit ups and finally laps around the field. As he jogged around, feeling a little breathless he looked at the others on the field.

Most were like him, more or less in shape. The young girl who had queried the press-ups had given up a while back and was sitting on the floor, her head in her hands. Artem was still chatting, this time to a group of women who were laughing at whatever it was he was saying. He caught Jed looking and give him two thumbs up. Despite himself, Jed smiled back.

Eventually, Archer blew a whistle to signify the end of the training session.

'Not bad,' she conceded. 'Some of you have clearly kept up with your fitness regime. Hit the showers, you'll be taken through the security of the Resistance base next.'

Jed jogged with the others to the building Archer had pointed at. He was relieved they weren't doing more physical training.

After sitting through a two-hour lecture on the security protocols for entering and exiting the Resistance base, Jed wished he was still running laps. Artem had actually fallen asleep and his snores rumbled through the classroom, causing a few of the others to giggle but the instructor didn't seem to notice. Only Archer was frowning at the slumbering Russian.

Finally, the instructor stopped talking and they were released from the stupefying atmosphere of the classroom to grab lunch before they were due to return for firearm evaluation.

In the mess hall, Jed was pleased to see Kira and the kids. He excused himself from the other trainees and went over to join her.

'Hey, hon.' He kissed the kids and then his wife on her cheek before sitting down next to her. 'How are you? Can I help?'

'We're fine. I got this' She smiled a small smile and went on feeding the two children by herself.

'Archer had us running laps this morning and then some instructor bored the socks off everyone with a lecture on security protocols.'

'Mmm hmm.'

Jed glanced at his wife. 'Then she gave us the keys to the castle and a rocket ship to the moon.'

'Yeah.'

'Kira? What's wrong?'

She glanced at him. 'Nothing, why?'

'I told you I was given a rocket ship to the moon.'

'Oh, sorry. I'm just tired. I'm okay.' She wiped the children's faces as they'd finished their lunch.

Jed looked at his wristplant, it was nearly time for him to go back. 'Look, if you need to talk, I'm here for you. I know what's like to lose family, remember.'

'I know, I will.'

Unconvinced, Jed gave her a hug and said goodbye

to the kids before hurrying back to training. Despite being concerned about Kira, he was looking forward to getting his hands on a firearm.

'Anyone used a weapon before?' asked Archer, sweeping her gaze up and down the line. About half the recruits stepped forwards, Jed and Artem included, she nodded. 'Right, you lot, stay here with me. The rest of you go inside and see Lieutenant Yarrow for basic handling.' She waited until the inexperienced trainees had gone before leading Jed and the others to the firing range.

There were various targets to aim for and the back wall was marked with laser burns, bullet holes and an arrow. Jed blinked in surprise. He hadn't expected that kind of weaponry.

'Okay, line up and you'll each be assessed on how well you can handle the laser gun.'

No-one seemed that keen on going first so Jed stepped forwards to the line and picked up the laser gun. It was Corporation issue but a few years old. Jed had been using the newer version on Force. He sighted the target, aimed and fired. Archer nodded but said nothing, gesturing for the next in line to step forward. Everyone shot the target.

'You've proven you can point and shoot. Congratulations,' said Archer drily. 'Unfortunately, we do not have a large store of laser guns and those we do have are old and prone to glitching. The Resistance were fortunate to discover an old weapons cache left behind from before The Event. We have been able to retro manufacture bullets. Let's see how well you can handle a real gun.' She looked at Jed. 'You'll need to wear the ear defenders for this.'

Jed was nervous but excited. He'd always wanted to

shoot a bullet gun after learning about them at Academy. He stepped up eagerly and put the ear defenders on. There was a pair of clear plastic glasses on the ledge too, so he donned those as well. Archer had moved closer to him in order to put her own protective gear on and gave him a quick run down of the weapon.

'Flick the safety off here, load the barrel here, aim at the dummy and fire. Watch out for the recoil.' She smiled slightly and waited for Jed to shoot.

He did as he asked and primed the gun. He used two hands to steady his aim and sighted along the barrel. Squeezing hard the gun fired throwing Jed's arms up with the force of shooting. The bullet flew way over the target and smacked into the wall at the back. Jed looked at the gun wonderingly. Clearly there was more skill involved in using one of these than the laser guns.

Archer was grinning. 'You only need to squeeze the trigger. Have another go. There are more bullets in the chamber.'

Jed refocused on the target. He was determined to get this right. This time he squeezed the trigger gently and the recoil lessened. He still missed the target but at least he hit the dummy. Smiling he put the gun down and stepped away from the firing zone.

'Not bad, rookie,' Archer gave him a brief smile and directed the next person in line up to the plate.

Jed stood back and watched the progress. Most people did the same as him and oversqueezed the trigger mechanism. There were a few cries of pain at bad recoil but otherwise no accidents. No-one made the target until it was Artem's turn. He moved up to the plate, picked the gun up with practised ease, checked the barrel was loaded and cocked the gun. He held in one handed, lifted his arm, sighted and made the shot. It was perfect. Jed whistled through his teeth, there was clearly more to the Russian than he'd given him credit.

'Excellent work, Misner. You can take over training the rest of them with the firearms. Let's move on.'

Jed frowned. *Move on to what?* He barked a laugh when Archer stopped at the far end of the range. There on the wall were a series of bows and arrows. 'You have got to be kidding me?' he said incredulously.

'I'm deadly serious. We will be teaching you how to make a bow and showing you how to make arrowheads. We don't just rely on the latest technology here at the Resistance.' Archer raised her voice to address the rest of them. 'As you all know, we are what is left. It's us and them. And New Corp are not interested in playing fair. We will not be able to stay here forever and searching for a new base, a new home may take us weeks. May take us months. The sea levels are rising and the more skills you have to survive out there, the better. Now, listen up.'

She went on to explain how to correctly hold the bow, where they should place their hands and how to pull the string back straight armed. She had them all practice their grip with and without arrows, and Jed was surprised to discover his arm shaking after keeping the bowline tense. When it came to shooting the arrows though it was a marked failure for everyone. Even Artem couldn't claim any skill in that department. When Archer called it a day, Jed was aching in places he didn't know could ache and he had a cracking bruise on his arm where the bowstring had slapped him soundly.

As they filtered back to the open training ground, Archer had them line up one more time. Those who had gone with Yarrow had also returned.

'This will be your new regime for the next couple of

weeks. You'll do fitness and a lecture before lunch then weapons training in the afternoon. If you feel you have a particular skill in a particular area, don't hold back, tell Yarrow and we'll see if we can use you. Remember, the Resistance finds a use for everything and everyone. Dismissed.'

Jed lingered for a moment to see if she had anything else to tell him, but as soon as people started to leave, she headed for the shower block. Artem clapped a hand on Jed.

'Come, comrade. Let us go eat and see how others did this day. There may be pudding.'

He sounded so hopeful that Jed couldn't help but grin and he followed his friend to the mess hall.

Chapter Thirteen

Dina and Ash left together after breakfast watched by Max, who was leaning on the kitchen counter.

'She is not interested, you know,' commented Martha, as she made sure she left Kira everything she needed to look after Lucas for the day.

'No? They seem to have a lot in common.'

'They do. That is why they are friends, but you do not have to worry about Ash. Dina is not his type.'

'She's smart, funny, caring. How can that not be his type?'

Martha shook her head, laughing. She leaned into Max.

'I assure you; Ash has no interest in Dina, or me, or any of the ladies here.' She waited a moment. Realisation dawned.

'Oh, she's not his type.' Max grinned. 'She's not his type. Excellent. Shall we go to the Allotment? Are you ready?'

Martha nodded. 'Yes. Let's go.' Then she stopped short and ran over to the play cube, where the children were, and gave her son a quick kiss on the head. 'Bye Kira,' she called softly before catching up with Max as he left the room.

When they arrived, there were several people milling around in front of the entrance.

'Must be the other new recruits,' whispered Max. 'Seems like there's quite a few of us.'

Bennett appeared. She had a dirty mark on one cheek and some foliage in her hair.

'Okay, you've all been assigned to Allotment. It's hard, dirty work but you're growing food for everyone in the Resistance so, if you ask me, there's no finer job. Anyone got any experience?'

There were a few raised hands, Max and Martha included.

'Right, you can come with me. The rest of you wait here. One of my gardeners will be along to teach you the basics.' She led the smaller group through the greenhouses, further than Max and Martha had been before. There was the odd person tending the plants here and there. It was very peaceful and serene. Bennett stopped outside a large building and swiped her arm to gain access. Inside were rows of plants seemingly floating in the air with their root systems dangling gracefully. They were suspended in special trays with a specialised air flow and water system supplying their needs.

'This is Fred,' said Bennett, waving her arm at a large computer screen with green swirls across its screen. 'It looks after the hydroponics, monitoring and adjusting the plants' needs automatically. We usually rota one gardener on a twelve-hour shift to keep an eye on things in here as well. The AI is not infallible.'

'Wow, they really like their AIs,' muttered Max under his breath to Martha.

Bennett overheard. 'Yes, Dr Carter, unfortunately we do have to rely on our AIs because there aren't enough of us to do everything. But everyone who works here is trained to use the hydroponics system without Fred, just in case.'

Max flinched at being addressed, surprised that Bennett remembered who he was.

'Will you be able to take the AIs with you? When the Resistance moves, I mean?' Martha peered to see who was talking. It was a short, bald man with glasses who was perspiring gently in the warm building.

Bennett flicked her eyes at the interactive screen before replying.

'You'd have to ask Archer about that. I deal in plants, not computers. Let's move on.'

The group filed out of the humid area, entering a small corridor.

'Don't be alarmed. We will now experience a decontamination spray prior to entering the seed bank.'

There was an excited murmur. Max bent down to Martha.

'This could be life changing. If they really do have a complete seed bank, just think of the different plants we could grow and the genetic applications that could be applied.' He had to stop speaking because of the decontamination spray but Martha shared his excitement. A fully stocked seed bank would be key to their future survival.

They stepped through not sure what to expect. It was a bit disappointing. There wasn't really anything to see. Rows and rows of metallic looking columns, each numbered. The room itself smelt of nothing. Another AI screen was available to their right. The swirling colours turned pale blue.

Welcome to the Seed Bank. How may I assist you?

'This is Layla. She looks after things in here and

over in the Tech labs. The environment is closely monitored to ensure the survival of our seeds. Hamble, ask Layla for something.'

Martha flushed at being put on the spot and tried to think of something she could ask for.

'Um... Layla, could I have some sunflower seeds, please?'

I am sorry, Gardener Hamble, but you do not have security clearance to request sunflower seeds.

Martha laughed awkwardly but felt embarrassed and moved closer to Max. He gave her a brief smile.

'As you can see, we have security protocols in place in case of any seed theft,' said Bennett.

'Why would anyone want to steal seeds?' asked a young man with rather large ears.

Bennett stared at him. 'The seeds in this bank are what we live on. They will be what we use to begin a new life somewhere else, should we move. If someone stole them, how would you eat? Developed some kind of resistance to radioactive plants, have you?'

'Er... no, I meant who would be mean enough to do that sort of thing?'

'Where are you from?' asked Bennett.

'City 5. There was a landslide, it knocked out our power and communications array. So we came here.'

Bennett sniffed. 'And did you try to get in touch with New Corp before you came here?'

'Of course, but...'

'But what?'

The boy's ears started to go very red and he blinked a few times. 'Well... they weren't really interested.'

'They turned you away because they didn't want to waste the resources going to collect you and bring you back to City 9. You would be a waste of their time and without the supplies of your city, a drain on theirs.'

'Now, wait a minute. That's a little harsh.' The boy tried to fight back. 'I'm sure they would've helped, if they'd known all the facts.'

Bennett frowned at him for a long moment. 'I don't want you in my gardens.' She touched a hand to an ear, activating a comm. 'Wilson, come and collect... sorry, what's your name?'

'David. David Malone,' said the bewildered lad.

'Come and collect Mr Malone from outside the seed bank. He requires reassignment and a full evaluation.'

Martha watched the exchange uneasily. It sounded like Bennett was getting rid of this David person because he didn't think like her. Which wasn't exactly the sort of attitude she'd been expecting from the Resistance. She risked a glance at Max and saw he was also frowning. This was definitely something she needed to speak to the others about. No-one spoke as Bennett ushered them all out of the seed bank, back through contamination into a small corridor.

There was a soldier was waiting for them.

'David Malone? Come with me, please.' Wilson was polite but also armed and had a no-nonsense air about him that meant no-one spoke up for the boy and they all watched him be escorted away.

Bennett clapped her hands to regain everyone's attention. 'Right, we have a series of experiments running plus the usual grunt work around the gardens for which you'll each be rota'd in for. We try to play to your strengths, but we are low on manpower so I'm afraid everyone swaps in on everything. You'll find your timetables in the hut. Come on, this way.' And she marched confidently away, in the opposite direction to Wilson and David.

The hut turned out to be just that. A large wooden hut with a series of long tables and chairs, a selection of wellington boots, gardening gloves, the odd tool and scraps of twine. There were a few plants on the window ledge, and everything smelt earthy.

'There's a kettle here, mugs etc. Try to wash up and replace, we don't have enough for you to be precious about them. Feel free to bring your own supplies in but be warned, there are biscuit thieves and it's completely at your own risk.' She didn't smile but there was a faint twinkle in her eye as she spoke.

'Now, usually lunch is up to you. You can bring it in, or you can go back to the Mess Hall, whatever. Today, we've put on sandwiches and that for you. So, enjoy!' Bennett swept an arm over to the far side of the room where there were several trays of food laid out.

The non-experienced people who had disappeared earlier were already there. Max and Martha hurried over to make sure they got a sandwich. They needn't have worried, there was plenty to go around.

'No sign of David,' whispered Max to Martha.

'No, I don't think we'll see him back here. I expect he'll be reassigned. Does it make you feel a bit...'

'Yeah, it does. I think we need to lie low and keep our eyes open.'

Martha chuckled at the thought of Max laying low, he was so tall he stood head and shoulders above everyone else there. He caught her looking up at him and smiled ruefully.

They began circulating and chatting with the others. Those with experience of working with plants had similar backgrounds to Martha and Max, but no-one seemed to have had as much hands-on growing experience as they had in City 42 and Camp Eden. It marked the two of them out. When most people had finished eating, Bennett reappeared with a collection of battered looking handhelds.

'These hold your rotas and a series of frequently asked questions. Check them first before you bother me, please. If you have your own, then you'll need to go to tech and get the apps from here moved over. We don't have that many to go around and the ones we do have, well, you can see for yourself the condition they're in.' Bennett glanced at her wristplant. 'Okay, check your rota and see where you should be then get gone. There's lots to do. Any problems, ask someone in green overalls who looks like they know what they're doing. There should be one or two around.' And she stomped off.

Martha checked her battered handheld.

'I'm on planting - you?'

Max checked, then grimaced. 'Weeding. My favourite. See you back here?'

She nodded and went to find the rows of planters she'd been working on the other day and found her assigned seeds waiting for her, together with a trowel. She spent the afternoon not really thinking about anything, focusing on putting a couple of seeds in each small hole, cover them over and watering as she went. Time marched by without her noticing and a claxon brought her out of her work.

'I guess that's the end of my shift,' she muttered to herself and stood up wincing as the muscles in her back complained. Her hands were engrained with dirt and all she wanted was to get back to their rooms and have a hot shower. One thing that was abundantly available was hot showers. She hurried to go find Max and return to Lucas and the others, all her doubts forgotten for the time being.

Chapter Fourteen

'This is so fragging cool!'

Ash grinned in response as he, Dina, and the other new recruits took a tour of the Science and Technology Division. A large hangar had been converted into multiple bays and each area of expertise occupied one of the bays. They'd seen robotics, attempts at recreating wristplant and handheld technology, adaptations to skimmers to make them run faster for longer as well as several other experiments Ash could only hazard a guess at.

'This is the last place to show you,' explained Veela, their guide. She was a willowy young woman with pale lilac hair and wore her silvery jumpsuit with confidence. 'This is where we monitor, update and generally try to keep an eye on our AI.' She peered into the workspace. 'Hmm, it looks like Dr Glover isn't in at the moment. She's the expert on the AIs.'

'You seem to rely on them a lot for everyday life,' commented Ash.

One of the people at the back of the group challenged Ash's statement. 'If you have the leading expert in the world on hand, it seems silly to ignore that expertise, don't you think?'

'Yeah, but artificial intelligence I mean, isn't that asking for trouble? New Corp have some great hackers and AIs can be cracked. They are only machines after all. Unless you've developed consciousness since you've been here, Dr Glover.' Ash grinned at the woman at the back of the group.

'MASH42 I presume?' The woman moved forward through the group, holding out her hand to Ash who took it and shook it enthusiastically. She kept hold of his hand and turned to speak to everyone. 'This here is the best hacker we have, hands down. If there is something you want to find out, he's your man.'

Dina was confused. *How did this woman already know who Ash was?* They'd only been with the Resistance a couple of days and she was fairly certain he hadn't hacked anything since they arrived.

Ash was starting to look uncomfortable at being in the limelight.

'Last I heard, you'd turned good cop working for Force?' asked Dr Glover.

Ash nodded but said nothing, unwilling to elaborate in front of the crowd. Dr Glover realised she was unnerving him, so she let go of his hand.

'Good to have you with us,' she said then addressed the others. 'Anyone got an area of expertise?'

A couple of hands raised, and voices called out several different fields of knowledge. 'Robotics.' 'Programming.' 'Engineering.'

'Excellent, we can make good use of all of that here. Veela, have you got the jacks?'

'Yes, Dr Glover.' The young woman reached into the satchel she wore slung across her body and handed one out to everyone. 'These jacks have all the details of what we're working on at the moment as well as the day-today jobs and repairs we get asked to do. You'll each get a turn working on the helpdesk, but when you're not there you're welcome to work on any of our projects, obviously ask the lead technician first. Oh, and if any of you have ideas for your own work, that's fine. You can pitch them to Dr Glover, and she'll decide whether we can spare the resources. It must be something that can help the Resistance now or in the future.'

Dr Glover nodded encouragingly at everyone. 'Yes, go back to your quarters, take the rest of the day to go through everything and decide what you want to do. Anyone who feels they'd be more useful elsewhere, see Lieutenant Kolwowsky and he'll assign you to housekeeping.' She caught Ash's eye, beckoning him over.

Dina hovered nearby not sure whether she should leave them to it or not. Dr Glover looked at her expectantly.

'Um, Dina, maybe you should wait for me back in our quarters. I won't be long.' Ash half smiled at her.

'Oh. Okay. If that's what you want. I'll, er... see you later.' And she walked away, feeling hurt at being left out of the conversation.

'I take it she doesn't know about your hacker days.'

'No. But you didn't have to be rude, sis.'

Dr Glover dropped the act and pulled her brother into a huge hug. 'It is so good to see you! Are you alright? Are you safe?'

Chapter Fifteen

Dina stalked all the way back to their quarters. At least she tried to, but she got lost twice refusing to use Lola to help her find her way back. She was too angry to have anything to do with Resistance right now. Ash knew one of the leaders in the Resistance. How had that never come up before? She was still fuming when she waved her arm at the doors to their residence. Nothing happened. She waved her arm again. A soft chime behind her made her whirl angrily.

Miss Grey, I am sorry to inform you that you are trying to enter barracks that have not been assigned to you or a member of your group. Please desist attempting to enter.

'Where the frag am I then?' Dina barked.

You are in corridor 3B.

'And where am I meant to be?'

I cannot answer that question, Miss Grey.

'Argh!' Dina screamed in frustration and kicked the wall. Lola did not respond. Taking a breath, Dina tried to think logically. 'Can you direct me to my quarters. Please.'

Of course. Please follow the yellow line. Have a pleasant day.

Standing in front of another set of identical looking doors, Dina hesitated. She didn't want to make a fool of herself again. Tentatively, she waved her arm and the doors slid open. She walked into Kira's meltdown.

'Why are you crying? I don't understand what you want! I've fed you, changed you, played with you and you are still screaming! AAAARRRRGGGGHHHHH!' Kira screamed at the top of her voice startling Dina and scaring the children. They stopped their crying momentarily only to begin wailing even louder.

'Whoa, Kira, calm down,' Dina said as she walked further into the room.

Kira threw her a frustrated look then dropped onto the sofa and began sobbing, her head in her hands.

Dina looked at the distraught children and her distressed friend. *Kids first* she thought.

'Alright, hey, it's alright. Aunty Dina is here. Hey, hey. It's alright. There, there. Come on, now.'

The children quietened at hearing Dina's calm voice and recognising her, but they were still hiccupping and taking shaky breaths because of how upset they had become. Dina tried to recall the checklist Martha had given her for watching Lucas before. She thought it went nappy, food, sleep, play but she remembered what Kira had just said. It sounded like the children had already been changed and fed. Instead she expanded the cube so that it was large enough for her to climb in too and she joined them. Instantly, three small bodies flung themselves at her and she ended up in a heaped hug. The babies were taking confidence from being close to each other and Dina as they all sat on the floor of the cube and she crooned wordlessly to them, stroking a head here and an arm there, breathing gently on the little ones cuddling her.

Eventually, the children grew calm enough to wander away from Dina to their favourite places in the play cube. Grace brought Dina back a soft toy and Peter pointed at a cartoon that was playing on the media screen. She switched the content to a lullaby and made sure all the kids had pacifiers and snuggle blankets. Originally, the others had scoffed at Kira for providing these old-fashioned devices to the children, but they had accepted them instantly and had grown attached to them. The babies snuggled into each other and slowly drifted off, the odd after-cry shudder here and there. Gradually, Dina extricated her foot from the bottom of the pile, careful not to wake the children and gently climbed back out of the cube.

Kira had stopped sobbing aloud but hadn't moved. Dina went to the kitchen and made some synth-caf. She brought two hot mugs over, put them on the table and sat as close to Kira as she could. Kira leaned into her friend slightly and mumbled a quiet thanks. They sipped their synth-caf for a few moments before Dina broached the subject.

'You want to talk about it?' she asked.

'Not really,' Kira replied.

Dina pursed her lips. 'How often does that happen?'

'What?' asked Kira.

'That.' Dina gestured towards the play cube. 'Total meltdown.'

'Ugh, that's the first time I've shouted at them like that.' She put her mug down. 'I'm so embarrassed. I can't believe you saw me like that. It's just… it's just, they never stop. It's constant all the time and you guys don't know what it's like because you swan in and swan out, doing your own thing and I'm left, literally holding the baby. Martha is like the perfect mum, working and looking after Lucas, and I can't even keep three children entertained without failing miserably.' Kira turned slightly to face her friend. 'All I want to do is talk to my mum and ask her advice on things and I can't even do that. She's gone.' Her bottom lip trembled, and she fought back the tears.

'You know you're not on your own though, right?' Dina asked. 'We're here for you. All of us.'

Kira smiled sadly. 'My sensible head knows you are, but it doesn't always feel like it. I feel so alone.'

The two women hugged, and Dina tried to think of the right thing to say, but before she had chance, Kira sat back and started speaking again.

'I mean, what are we actually doing here? Are we joining the Resistance? Are we fighting New Corp? Again? It seems like such a waste of time. Does anyone really believe that this little band of misfits really stands a chance against the might of New Corp? They killed my parents, Dina. They killed Ruth. And baby Sarah. Yes, they deserve to be punished for that but is being here the best way to do that? I'm not sure. Nobody here seems to give a frag about what happened.'

Dina shifted on the sofa. 'What else are we supposed to do? There's nowhere else to go. I think… look, I don't know what the best thing to do is Kira, really, I don't. I think we need to keep our eyes and ears open while we are here.' Dina started to bite her nails.

'Why what happened?' prompted Kira.

'It's Dr Glover, the head of Science and Technology. She knew Ash from before somehow. She knew he was a hacker and said he was the best around. How did she know who he was?'

Kira shrugged. 'Maybe she's a hacker too. They do tend to move in the same circles, don't they?'

'I guess, but…' Dina was interrupted as Ash returned to their quarters.

'Hi guys!' He had a huge smile on his face and completely missed the serious tone of the room. He nodded at their cups. 'Any left?' But didn't wait for an answer and went into the kitchen to pour himself a cup of synth-caf. He was busy browsing his handheld at the same time. 'I'm gonna go check out the different projects S and T are working on. Try and figure out what I want to do.' He grinned at them again and went into his room happily.

'He seems happy,' remarked Kira. 'At least one of us is.'

They didn't have the chance to continue their conversation as first Jed and Artem, then Martha and Max returned from their own assignments. Dina tried to catch Jed.

'Jed, look, there's something off about Dr Glover,' she began.

Jed's stomach rumbled loudly. 'Look, why don't we all report back after dinner? I'm starving and I'm not going to be able to concentrate until I've had something to eat. That way everyone can have their say about who they met and where they went, rather than having to repeat ourselves. What do you think?'

'I guess,' Dina conceded but she wasn't happy about it.

'Why do we all have to have our meals in the mess hall? Don't you think it's a bit weird?' Kira asked to the room in general, but everyone was too busy getting themselves sorted to go to dinner that no-one replied to her. 'Well, I think it's weird. Come on, Grace.'

Despite Jed's suggestion that people waited until after dinner to talk about what they seen and heard, everyone was chattering animatedly on the way to dinner and as they took their seats at an empty table. There was a vat of vegetable soup and crusty rolls with some cheese and fruit on the table. Nobody said much as everyone tucked in.

'Alright, guys?' said Kolwowsky as he passed by. Jed gave him a nod and a wave, but the soldier didn't stop to say anything else.

Dr Glover walked by and squeezed Ash's shoulder as he passed causing Dina to glower at her, pushing her half-eaten soup to the middle of the table, her appetite ruined. She waited impatiently for everyone to hurry up and finish eating so she could get started on grilling Ash.

'Okay, we've all survived our first day in Resistance. Everyone alright?' Jed asked, back in their quarters. There were murmurs and nods. 'Artem and I had physical training, lectures on security protocols and weapons training. Archer was in charge although she didn't deliver the lectures. Apparently, that's what we can look forward to for the near future. A mixed bag of personnel, wasn't it, Artem?'

'Da,' the Russian nodded. 'Some shooters, some not so much but more Russians means more vodka!' And he flourished a bottle of alcohol, laughing as he set it on the table.

'Maybe after everyone's checked in, Artem,' chuckled Jed. 'Martha, Max, how was Allotment? What's Bennett like?'

'It's good, they seem to have things well under control. There's AI in there as too, Fred and Layla but, Bennett doesn't seem to be much of a fan. I think she tolerates their presence because she has to. They have a complex hydroponic system which Fred monitors, a highly secure Seed Bank that Layla controls, and then there are all the external greenhouses and planters. They're short on manual labour and supplies are a little rudimentary in places but Bennett definitely knows her stuff. She's also not shy about... well, she got rid of someone for voicing sympathy for New Corp,' said Max, looking at Martha for confirmation.

She nodded. 'Yes, it was a bit odd, to be honest. I do not know what happened to the boy, maybe he will be reassigned somewhere. I do not think they will get rid of him permanently. Will they?' Martha asked uncertainly, looking at the group.

There were several shrugs and headshakes, but no one knew for sure.

'Maybe we could ask Kolwowsky, he seems to know what's going on. More or less,' suggested Kira.

'Yeah, maybe,' agreed Jed.

'Bennett is someone I wouldn't cross in a hurry. She knows her own mind and is fiercely protective of Allotment. She's not afraid to say what she thinks, and she doesn't think very much of the AIs or of Zac apparently.' Max laughed nervously. 'To be fair, I don't think she thinks very much of anyone.'

Martha chuckled and nodded her agreement. Jed waited a moment to see if they had any more to say before moving things on.

'Ash, Dina, you're up.'

'Layla, the AI, helps run Science and Technology too, and there are tons of exciting projects to work on, I have no idea what to choose,' said Ash enthusiastically.

'How many AI is that now then? Four?' asked Jed to the group. The others nodded. 'Frank in stores, Fred and Layla in Allotment, Lola in the corridors and then Layla again in Science and Technology as well as the Seed Bank. Seems a bit odd to have so many, doesn't it?'

'It's because Dr Glover is apparently an AI expert. She also seems to know an awful lot about you, doesn't she, Ash?' Dina challenged.

Artem barked a laugh. 'Of course she does. Is sister!'

Everyone stared at the Russian in surprise before turning their attention to Ash who was blushing furiously.

Chapter Sixteen

'Your sister?' exclaimed Dina. 'Since when?'

'How did you know, Artem?' asked Jed at the same time but the Russian just smiled and sat back, letting Ash explain.

'Um.' Ash scratched his head and looked at the people in front of him. He was met with stern faces. Except for Artem.

'What the frag, Ash?' demanded Dina. 'What's going on?'

'I'm from City 1, originally,' he replied but Martha interrupted him.

'The one that was set up to be as much as possible like Earth used to be?' she asked.

'Yes, that's right. I was in the foster system; I never knew my parents. They died in some accident or radiation poisoning or something. No one really knows. Orphans were quite common.' He glanced around the group. 'You have to understand that the people who wanted City 1 to be the way it was had shunned Corporation involvement. They thought the other cities of survivors should all be set up the same way, like them, but Corporation disagreed. They thought the other cities should be regulated and controlled. Different experiments running in each. There were disagreements and eventually City 1 lost its influence and Corporation were too powerful to stop. They moulded the other cities into what they wanted them to be.'

'Why did you never share this information before, Ash?' asked Jed. He was shocked at what little he knew.

'I told Chief Minkov when I arrived in City 42. He told me to keep it to myself.' Ash shrugged. 'I thought he would've told you. Sorry.'

Jed nodded and gestured for Ash to continue.

'Dr Glover, Jess, was my foster sister. We grew up together in the system. I tried to keep in touch with her, but we lost contact a while back.'

'How did you know, Artem?' asked Kira. 'Why didn't you tell us?'

'I had information files on everyone. Part of my job for Resistance. I thought you knew.' He was entirely unapologetic.

'Why did you leave City 1?' Martha asked Ash. 'And how did you end up in City 42?'

'There was an outbreak of 'flu and not many survivors. That's why City 1 fell. It was outside the protection of Corporation and left to fend for itself. I didn't plan to come to City 42, it's just how it happened. A series of events led me there.'

'*A series of events*? You expect us to believe that?' Dina was still fuming.

'Hey, things happened. I drifted a bit. Different cities had different computer systems and when I hacked into networks and saw that Corporation had a greater presence in City 42 but wasn't as Corp heavy as City 9, I thought it might be a good place to survive.' He spread his hand out in defence. 'I was young.'

'Did you get caught, as a hacker, I mean?' asked Jed.

'Yes. That's how I ended up in front of the Chief. He told me I had a choice. I could either join Force and work for him or I could say goodbye to my freedom and become a prisoner of Corporation.'

'He specifically asked you to work for him?' Jed wanted to clarify the point.

'Yes. He didn't trust Corporation.'

'That wiley old fox knew something was going to happen, always tried to be one step ahead.' Jed shook his head, fondly remembering his old chief.

'I took his offer, became an operative and worked in Force for a while before getting assigned to your team, Jed. I never spied on anyone. I don't work for New Corp, I never have, I swear.'

'We believe you,' said Kira gently. 'I just wish you'd told us your background.'

'I honestly thought Jed already knew. I'm sorry.'

'What about Glover then? Where did she go? Why wasn't she in City 42 with you?' demanded Dina. She wasn't satisfied and wanted more answers.

'We split up after leaving City 1. She wanted to go a different way to me. I thought there would be more for us in City 42, she disagreed. We left on good terms, though and always said we would try and connect when we could. I haven't heard from her for a while.'

'But you knew she was here?' queried Dina.

'I knew she had joined the Resistance. But I didn't know where she was exactly. We haven't spoken recently, and I haven't seen her for a long time.' Ash looked at the doubtful faces. 'Guys, you have to believe me, I'm with you. I thought I was part of your team. I didn't mention Jess because I honestly thought the Chief had shared my background with you, Jed. I have never lied to any of you.'

'An omission of fact is as bad as a downright lie,' muttered Dina, feeling hurt that her friend Ash hadn't confided in her earlier.

Max frowned at her and held his hand out to Ash. 'I believe you and I trust you. Perhaps you can invite your sister over one evening so we can all get to know her better.'

Ash grabbed Max's hand and shook it enthusiastically. 'That would be great. I know she'd love to get to know you all.'

Jed pulled the discussion back to the Resistance. 'How many people did you see today, while you were on assignment, Martha?'

'Not that many, maybe fifty,' she replied, looking at Max to confirm. He nodded in agreement.

'Yeah, same in Science and Technology. About fifty or so,' said Dina, still miffed at Ash not telling her he had a sister.

'Me too. Not that many, really. And we've never seen more than a couple of hundred in the Mess Hall.' Jed ran his hand through his hair. 'I think they're telling the truth you know, about there not being that many people left.'

'I agree,' said Martha. 'I feel that Zac would not lie to us about this. It is too important.'

'What do you think the Resistance is after?' asked Kira.

'I don't know,' replied Jed honestly. 'The salvation of the human race might sound a bit high and mighty, but I really believe they want to make a safe place for the people they have gathered here, away from New Corp.'

'What do we do now?' asked Max.

'Drink!' exclaimed Artem who had gone to find glasses for the vodka. It broke the tense mood and most of the friends laughed.

'I think we need to keep our heads down and our eyes and ears open. It feels a little too good to be true at the moment. Keeping our family safe has to be the priority,' said Jed and the others murmured their agreement.

Artem poured the shots and lifted his own glass. 'To us!' he threw the shot back.

'To us!' the others said as they followed his example.

Chapter Seventeen

'How are the new arrivals settling in?' Zac asked as his team met together for a synth-caf. He didn't like to think of it as a formal meeting, more of a general get together.

'Fine,' replied Bennett, already looking at her wristplant, keen to be away from the meeting.

'Yep, it's great to have some fresh ideas and of course, as you know, my brother Matt is one of the new arrivals,' said Dr Glover, smiling around the room as she spoke.

'Matt?' queried Zac, then he thought for a moment. 'Oh, you mean Ash. Is that his first name? Wait… he's your brother?'

Glover laughed and nodded as Zac whistled in surprise.

'Wow, I'm glad we've been able to reunite you guys.'

'I know, it's great. I knew he'd ended up in City 42, but I had no idea he would make it over here to join us. He's going to be such an asset,' she replied.

'Can he be trusted though?' asked Archer. 'Can we trust anyone from that place?'

'I think so,' said Zac. 'But you've seen them in action, some of them anyway. How was peacekeeping?'

'It was as expected. Most people don't know their ass

from their elbow when it comes to using anything other than a point and shoot laser. And most people can't even handle that simple weaponry.' She snorted as she remembered the weapons training. 'Interestingly, Jed and Artem – the two people from City 42 - were adept, even in archery. Especially the Russian.'

'You know Artem is on our side, Archer.'

'Hmm.' She took a long swallow of her synth-caf. 'I still think we should be keeping a very close eye on the lot of them.'

'I got rid of someone,' said Bennett, enjoying the shocked silence that followed her statement.

'When you say got rid…' enquired Zac tentatively.

'I had someone from security reassign the little toe rag. He was spouting some nonsense about Corporation or New Corp or whatever they're calling themselves these days. He was saying maybe they're not that bad. I wanted him out of my seed bank there and then. I will not compromise my seeds.' Bennett's nostrils were flaring, and her eyes looked accusingly at Zac.

'I agree that the seed bank must be kept safe, but I have been wondering whether we should extend the hand of friendship to the citizens of City 9 and City 42. What do you think?' Zac waited to see what the others would say.

There was a pause before all three women replied, 'No!' emphatically.

'You can't trust them, they'll try and take our tech, bug our systems. What about our AI?' said Glover.

'I am not letting a single one of them anywhere near my seeds. It's not happening,' fumed Bennett.

'It's too much of a security risk, Sir. You have to see that.' Archer was frowning as she looked intently at Zac.

'I realise that it might not be the most popular

choice...'

'*Might* not be? Are you mad?' Bennett was nearly apoplectic.

'Look, the people on that island are just that, people. I'm not going to be the head of the Resistance and not offer the same freedoms to everyone.' Zac surveyed the room. 'You've seen the reports. You know what's going to happen. People are going to die. We cannot save everyone and that's a hard fact to have to swallow. But we might be able to at least save some of them.'

There was no reply and Zac sighed heavily.

'I know it's not a great idea, believe me, I understand your reticence but... I think we have to try.'

'You should put it to the vote,' said Archer, flicking her eyes at the other two women. 'Everyone has to agree. New Corp have hurt a lot of people.'

Glover was nodding. 'But there are still innocents in those cities, and they deserve the chance for a better life. A chance at survival. I agree with Archer, put it to the vote.'

'You know what that means though, don't you?' asked Bennett.

'What?' Zac was bemused.

'If the resistance say no, then you have to let those people go.'

Zac pursed his lips a little, ready to argue then realised she was right. He couldn't expect the Resistance to only do what he thought was right. It made him no better than New Corp.

'Okay, a vote then. We'll give everyone a chance to decide what we should do.'

There was another silence as people finished their drinks. Bennett was the first to stand up and leave. She muttered a gruff goodbye and stomped out of the room, back to her precious plants.

'I'd better get back to work, we have lots to do if we want to take the AI with us when we move and now that I have some more brainpower down there, I think we should have a solution soon,' said Glover. She smiled warmly as she put her mug down. 'Thank you for bringing Matt, Ash, back to me.' She pecked Zac on the cheek as she left, startling him so much he nearly dropped his own mug.

Archer snorted in amusement as Zac recovered.

'Is there anything else?' he asked.

'I still think we should keep an eye on the newest arrivals, the ones you brought back from 9. I don't know that I trust where their loyalties lie. And as for Artem…'

'I vouch for Artem,' said Zac swiftly. 'He's loyal to the Resistance. I know he is.'

Archer shrugged. 'If you say so, Sir.' She put her mug down and paused at the doorway. 'Promise me you'll keep your eyes open though, just in case.'

'I promise,' said Zac, smiling at his second-in-command. 'Everything will work out, you'll see.'

Chapter Eighteen

The next morning, Kira woke feeling resolute. 'I'm going to speak to Zac.'

'Yeah? What about?' Jed was getting ready for his second day of training and couldn't decide if he was or wasn't looking forward to it.

'Staying in here with the kids is driving me up the wall. I want something to do. Maybe I could help at the school. I think Grace, and the others, would benefit from some extra interaction and stimulus.' She gazed round the room. 'There is literally nothing for me to do here.'

Jed smiled at his wife. 'That's great, hon. I've been really worried about you and everything that has happened. I agree, you need something to get your teeth into but be prepared to be disappointed. You might not even get in to speak to him.'

'We'll see. Come on, let's go get breakfast.'

They joined the others and strolled over to the mess hall, but instead of the usual selection of food available there were dry ration sachets, rehydrated with water. None of them were particularly appetising.

'Why are we eating this?' asked Dina in dismay, she had been hoping for pancakes.

'I guess there must be a supply issue, or something?'

Ash was looking around, trying to see if he could see his sister anywhere but there was no sign of her.

'Look, there's Kolwowsky. Let's ask him.' Dina waved to get the Lieutenant's attention. He waved back but hurried off in the opposite direction. 'Huh, that's strange.'

They ate the rations without enthusiasm, and it didn't take long before the meagre meal had gone.

'I guess we should go to our assigned work placements?' Martha was feeling uneasy.

'Yes, you should. I'll take Lucas with me. I'm going to talk to Zac about the school. He'll have a great time.' Kira was smiling, trying to look more confident than she felt.

'Yes, we'd better go, Ma.' Max was already on his feet, checking his wristplant. 'I wouldn't like to see Bennett in a bad mood.' He smiled to show he was mostly joking.

'Yeah, we'd better go to Science and Technology I suppose. I want to talk to your sister, Ash.' Dina had a determined look on her face. She wanted some answers.

'Okay, have a great day, guys.' Kira kissed her husband and pushed the expanded stroller out of the mess hall. All three children were happily chuntering away, looking at their surroundings and content after having had breakfast.

She knew vaguely where she wanted to go, but to make sure she touched one of the wall panels to access Lola.

Hello, Mrs Jenkins. How may I assist you?

'Can you direct me to Zac's office, please? I mean General Ridgely.'

General Ridgely is not currently in his office. Would you like me to guide you to where he currently is?

'Yes, please, Lola. That would be great.'

Please follow the yellow line. Have a pleasant day.

Feeling confident, Kira walked in the direction the yellow line on the wall was directing her. It led her through corridors she hadn't yet been down and past some empty laboratories. There were less and less people the further she walked, and she started to feel on edge.

Turning the corner into another corridor she noticed one of the light fixtures was broken and there were several burn marks on the wall. Kira touched one lightly with a finger.

'Is that a laser burn?' she wondered aloud.

The yellow line was telling her to go through a set of exterior double doors. She pushed them open cautiously and found herself in a wildly overgrown garden.

There, talking to the air was Zac. Kira moved closer to see if she could hear what he was saying. As she rounded the corner, she was first elated then dismayed to see a blue shimmer. Before it faded away, Kira was able to make out the shape of a woman with glowing blue skin. It was Gaia but then she was gone.

Zac spun on his heel, one hand on his weapon as he realised there was someone there,

'Don't shoot!' joked Kira but her heart was pounding out of her chest as she positioned herself in front of the travel cub, in an effort to protect the children.

'What are you doing here?' demanded Zac.

'Looking for you. Was that Gaia?'

Zac nodded. 'She comes here sometimes but she never says anything. Just looks sadly at me. I talk to her, try to clear my head.'

'May I?' Kira gestured towards where Zac was standing. As he nodded and moved away, Kira checked on the children. They were snoozing. She parked the stroller and walked over to the spot.

As she stood where he had been, the blue shimmer appeared again. A faded Gaia who did indeed look sadly at her. Kira peered at the image. Then looked around. She walked forward quickly, and the image wobbled as she walked through it.

'Hologram.'

'What?' Zac took a step forward.

'It's a hologram. There are projectors... here and over here.' Kira bent down to show Zac where the projectors were hidden under the overgrown gardens. 'Someone did indeed see Gaia and record her, but I don't think you've been talking to the real thing.'

Zac scuffed his shoe on the floor, shoulders slumped. 'I thought, I thought she was on our side. I thought the fact that she showed herself every time I came to see her was a good omen. What a fool.'

'You're not a fool. I'm sure she heard your prayers even though she wasn't here herself. Don't be so hard on yourself.'

Zac nodded, clearly disappointed but trying to put a brave face on it. 'Did you want me for something?'

'Yeah um, I wanted to talk to you about having something to do. Maybe in the school or...' She shrugged. 'Anywhere I can be useful really.'

'What about them?' Zac nodded to the children.

'We'd have to work something out, obviously.'

'Come on, let's go back to my office. At least there's some real coffee there.'

'Don't you have meetings? Things to do?'

'Probably, but I doubt the whole camp will fall apart if I stop to have coffee with someone who has actually seen Gaia. Maybe you can give me some advice.' He held the door open for her and they left the gardens behind them.

'Can I ask a question?'

'Of course. I'll try and answer.' Zac looked down at the floor as they walked along.

'Why was the menu so radically different this morning? In the mess hall, I mean, for breakfast.'

'Hmm. Well, to be blunt, we've had a large influx of new people and we wanted to impress you with what we have but apparently, Frank...'

'The AI?'

'Yes, the AI in stores. Frank has shut down non-essential purchasing and unfortunately dried food sachets is what we get left with.' He glanced up at Kira's face. 'Don't worry, things will even out. More workforce will mean we can ease workloads and get things finished faster. In fact, Dr Glover is working on some replicator technology that will be able to make whatever you want to eat.'

'That sounds almost impossible.'

'It's something to do with the molecular configuration of items or something. I'll admit my strengths don't lie in science.'

Kira smiled. 'Where do your strengths lie then?'

'Um, hopefully in leading the Resistance?' Zac frowned slightly as he spoke.

'No, I meant - what's your passion? What do you love to do?'

'Oh, I see. Er... do you know, Kira, I haven't got a clue anymore.' He laughed self-consciously. 'They made me General here mostly because I've been here the longest, I think. I don't have any military qualifications. All this rank and file business is a bit beyond me to be honest.'

'So why do you keep doing it then? Why not open up the decision-making process to the rest of the people here.'

'They tried that, the ones that came before my parents. They tried to lead collectively but the thing is, Kira, people don't function very well when everyone is trying to be the chief. We need someone to tell us what to do, if only so we can grumble about it the entire time.'

They had arrived at Zac's office; he opened the door for her and waited while she wheeled the children inside. They had woken up and Grace was beginning to get cross. She wanted to get out of the cube and explore.

'I can get them something to eat maybe, if they'd like?' Zac offered.

'It's alright, I brought things with me. Just a minute.' Kira unpacked three bottles and a snack box for the children. She placed the box in the middle of the cube and activated its magnetic connection so the children would be unable to throw the box around, hoping they would be distracted by food and change their mind about getting out. It worked.

'That's pretty nifty,' observed Zac.

'We were lucky. We packed our baby gear when we were on diplomatic mission, when we thought we were still part of City 42.' Kira fell quiet and Zac busied himself making the coffee he'd promised.

'I can put a word in with the school, if that's what you want. I'm sure they'd be grateful of the help. I think it's a bit of a mixed bag over there if I'm honest. A range of ages and not that much in the way of resources.'

'We'll have to teach like our ancestors did then.'

'How do you mean?' Zac was intrigued.

'By telling stories and getting them to learn things by rote. Hands on experience, that sort of thing. I'm sure the

Allotments and the Science and Technology Department won't be averse to having some willing helping hands from time to time.'

'You can ask Bennett.'

Kira laughed. 'Are you scared of her too?'

'Have you met her?'

Kira shook her head, still laughing when the door chimed and announced Colonel Archer.

'Apologies for interrupting, Sir.' Archer didn't look remorseful at all. 'There's a situation that needs your attention.'

'I'm very sorry, Kira. We'll have to continue our conversation another time. Ask Lola to take you to the school.' Zac smiled a warm smile in her direction before visibly pulling on his mantle of the Resistance General and assuming leadership once more.

Colonel Archer watched Kira with narrowed eyes, as she manoeuvred the travel cube out of Zac's office and left the room.

'Oh, it's not me you have to worry about, love,' muttered Kira under her breath, thinking she must tell Martha that she thought someone else was romantically interested in Zac. Although she didn't know whether Martha still was now that she'd found out Zac was leader of the Resistance. Kira made a mental note to tell her mum the gossip, forgetting for a moment that she was gone. Remembering made her catch her breath in a sudden bout of grief and her good mood evaporated. She'd ask Lola to take her to the school tomorrow. Now all she wanted to do was cry.

Chapter Nineteen

'What's the emergency, Archer?'

'Glover managed to hack into the satellites. We have real time imagery for the coastlines. It doesn't look good.'

'What about the recon teams we sent to cities 20 and 43, have they come back yet?'

'No, we heard from 20 and they found the city deserted. Either the inhabitants already decided to leave, or New Corp got there first.'

'Is that likely?'

'They wiped out 15, Sir, and 41 which should've been a logistical nightmare for them. If indeed they are only based in City 9.'

'I saw no convincing evidence of that while I was there, Archer,' replied Zac. 'There's no doubt that City 9 is a corper city but other than a large force of security officers, I didn't see any other official presence. There certainly weren't any leaders based there.'

'Even so, Sir. They have to have their base of operations somewhere.'

'Glover hasn't had any luck backtracking yet then?'

'No, but she's hopeful that with that hacker here, Ash something, she'll have better luck.'

'You know he's her brother? From City 1?'

Archer raised an eyebrow but didn't comment.

'I thought we'd lost track of all the City 1 evacuees. Interesting that one has turned up after all this time, don't you think?' Zac didn't think he had anything to fear from Ash and his connection with Glover, but he hadn't been pleased to learn about it when Artem had given him the backgrounds for everyone that had travelled with him. Something else to worry about. He backtracked.

'What about the other recon team that went to 43, headed by Simmonds, wasn't it?'

'Yes, Sir. No news yet, Sir.'

Zac stopped walking causing Archer to nearly run into him.

'I'm sure she's fine,' he said with a hand on her arm.

Archer flushed and half smiled, her professional facade slipping for a moment.

'Of course, Sir. I do too, Sir.' And her guard was back.

Zac sighed and started walking again.

'Did you say the satellite images are real time?'

'Yes, Sir.'

They arrived at the briefing room and Zac was pleased to see Glover was already there. Ash and Dina stood behind her.

'Are they fully cleared?' Archer nodded at the two unexpected additions.

'I vouch for them,' Dr Glover said stepping forward. 'Here are the latest images. As you can see landmass has shrunk much faster than we expected. If it continues at this rate, we will have to move up our evacuation plans.'

'How long do we have?' asked Zac peering at the maps up on the screen.

'I'd say a matter of weeks, but I'd rather not leave it

until the last minute.'

'Are your AIs portable?'

'Not yet but with my two newest recruits, I've made that our highest priority.' Glover smiled at Ash and Dina.

'So, the big question now is do we share what we know with New Corp and offer them the chance to join us,' mused Zac.

'You cannot be serious?' asked Dina, brushing off Ash's attempts to hush her.

'I'm looking at a possible mass extinction event, Miss Grey. I want to save as many lives as possible.'

'They murdered City 15. They killed Kira's parents. Ruth and her baby. You can't hand them an olive branch like nothing happened.'

'That is not my intention. Yes, soldiers of New Corp did atrocious things but until we can prove otherwise, I have to assume they were acting under orders. The sort of unquestioning loyalty I would expect from Resistance soldiers. What about the citizens of City 9? Would you hold them accountable for the actions of those in power? Do they even know what happened?'

'No, probably not, but ignorance is not an excuse.'

'That's a very hard line, Miss Grey.' Zac turned away to look at the maps once more. 'Archer, call a general meeting. We need to let everyone know the timetable has moved and that I want to put the olive branch evac option to the vote. Let us see what everyone else thinks we should do. Thank you, Dr Glover. Keep me updated.' He smiled at them all then left the room.

Archer rounded on Dina.

'You should show him some respect,' she snapped as she swept out after him.

'Huh. I'd better let Ma know she has some competition,' Dina muttered.

'Oh no, she's not interested in him that way. She's just very loyal. Come on, you two. We have work to do.' Dr Glover led the way back to Tech.

'If we still had the functional power of the internet, I would release the AIs into the nether space, and we could collect them when we arrive wherever it is we're going to arrive but I don't think there's enough power.' Dr Glover was thinking aloud and seemed startled when Dina asked a question.

'Do you have live internet here then?'

'Of course we do, after a fashion. It's what the AI's live on and communicate with. It's how we run our internal communication system.'

'So why can't you set up an infrastructure wherever we're going to be and link in that way. It's not like you need to run a cable all the way from here to there. Is it?' asked Dina.

'No, but if New Corp destroy our base before we get there, we run the risk of losing everything. We have to transfer the AIs manually,' explained Glover.

'Okay, surely the technology already exists to put them on a yottabyte drive or something?'

Dr Glover smiled. 'Yes, but it's the interface that we need to try and keep. Putting Layla onto a thumb drive is like saying we're going to give you a lobotomy. Everything will still be there, but you won't work quite the same way.'

Dina frowned. 'So, it's an interface issue - can't you downsize the existing screens and components? Turn them into miniature versions of themselves? That way you can rescale them back up when we get to wherever it is we're going.'

'You know, that's not such a bad idea.' Glover opened up her touch pad and tapped in some calculations.

Ash nudged Dina and gave her a thumbs up. He was pleased they were getting along.

Dina grinned in spite of herself. Having a problem to solve made her feel less annoyed at having been kept in the dark about Ash and his sister.

Chapter Twenty

'Order! Order! Can I please have a bit of quiet?' Zac called out over the general hubbub in the room. He had called a meeting for everyone to attend and had decided to hold it in the mess hall, after dinner, so that no-one had any excuse not to be there.

'HEY!' roared Artem making those closest to him jump as the room feel silent in surprise. 'Is important.' He turned and nodded towards Zac giving him the floor.

'Thanks, Artem. I have a critical announcement and we, the Resistance, have a decision to make. You will all receive the details on your info boards in your quarters later but to summarise, the sea levels are rising faster than we anticipated. We need to bring forward our evacuation and resettlement to higher ground.'

'To when?' called a voice from the crowd.

'End of next week,' replied Zac.

There was a stunned silence before everyone began shouting at once.

'You can't be serious?'

'Next week?' Do we even know where we are going?'

'How are we going to move everyone?'

'What's the rush? Why can't we stay here?'

Zac held up his hands for silence, but again it was a loud whistle from Artem that quietened the room.

'According to the satellite imagery we were able to obtain, we have already identified a place, not that far from here, which is high enough above sea level to be safe and large enough to accommodate us all. Initial contact has already been made and I will be sending an advance party to confirm the location's suitability before the entire camp is broken down and moved. We may have less time than we thought but we still have enough time to be safe.'

'What's the name of this magical place?' someone asked.

'It's City 50.'

The room erupted again.

'Why is everyone so angry about City 50?' Kira asked Jed but he shrugged. He had no idea.

Artem had overheard.

'City 50 is where babies went.'

'What?' Kira was confused for a moment then realised what Artem meant. The babies that had been grown secretly at City 42 and sent away. 'Who owns the city?'

'Is New Corp or was. Listen.'

Zac was speaking again.

'City 50 is the pinnacle of New Corp - the best technology, the best people, the best location. The city was built in the least affected area from radiation. It has a fresh water supply; they farm the land and grow supplies.'

'How do you know all this?' Dina called out.

'Because I have been there.'

'Is it where they have been sending all the babies from City 42?' Martha asked. She'd been listening to

Kira and Artem's conversation.

'Yes. And the families there are extremely grateful. They, like the rest of us, were affected by the HER and resulting sterility. They, like the rest of us, were duped by Corporation into thinking that sterility was permanent,' Zac explained.

'But why are we going to them? Surely that puts us back under New Corp control?' someone else called out.

'This is a signed treaty between me and the leader of City 50.' Zac held up something white and flimsy.

'It's a piece of paper,' whispered Kira as another voice shouted the very same thing.

'Yes, it is a piece of paper. I also have it in electronic format, but the fact remains that the leader of City 50 was willing to come to the table for the good of humanity. To see the survival of the entire human race and not squander anymore precious lives. All of you have been given a full report that you can read later. Anyone who doesn't want to come, doesn't have to but please, don't let prejudice affect your decision.'

The room had quietened to a buzz as people were talking quietly in small groups.

'There is one more thing we need to decide. Before we evacuate our base, should we extend the hand of peace to the citizens of City 42 and 9?' Zac barely managed to finish his sentence before the room erupted once more. He looked helplessly at Archer, who gave him a told-you-so look. People had begun to approach the podium, clamouring to be heard and to ask questions. Zac went down to the floor and began doing his best to answer queries. He found himself shoulder to shoulder with Martha, who had begun to field questions about City 42 and calm some of the people down. He smiled at her gratefully and together they tried to quell the storm.

Kira roped Dina and Max into helping her get some food and drink handed round to people while Jed, Ash and Artem tried to sooth people's fears.

As Kira handed Zac a cup of synth-caf he caught her arm for a second.

'Thank you, for this. You're really calming everyone down.'

She regarded him for a moment. 'You dumped a lot of information on them all at once, they need to process it.'

Martha joined them. 'I agree, if you want people to make an informed decision about what they do next, they need some time to read the information and digest everything.'

Zac nodded and headed back up to the top of the podium. He clapped his hands together loudly a couple of times.

'Can I have your attention? Everyone, please. This is what we're going to do. Please take some time to go back to your quarters, have a read through of the information you've all been sent. Ask questions. Talk amongst yourselves, decide what you want to do - what you think we should do.' He paused to look out across the room. 'We are very nearly all that's left. Let's make the right decision. We'll meet back here tomorrow, and you can cast your vote.'

This time there was no hubbub. People drifted off back to their quarters or jobs or wherever they needed to be.

'Thank you for your help, all of you.' Zac re-joined Kira, Martha and the others. 'I hope I handled that the best way I could.'

'You did what you could with the information you have. You were honest, up to a point. Admitting to keeping back the details of City 50 was maybe not the best idea.' Martha was trying to be supportive, but she was disappointed that Zac had hidden yet another secret from her.

'When did you go there?' asked Jed. 'Do you have any images or information I could look at?'

'It's all on the info package we sent out to everyone. I was there before I went to City 9. I had hoped I would be able to broker a similar deal over there, but it was clear to me as soon as I arrived that City 9 was a total Corper city.'

'And you didn't get that vibe from City 50? Despite the reputation New Corp has?' Jed was intrigued.

'It's like City 1 was meant to stand for the old ways and City 50 stands for the new way. I believe that way is not Corp or Resistance. I believe it's just us.' Zac half smiled at them as he turned away, flanked as always by Archer. There were other people waiting to speak to him.

'What do you make of all that, then?' Dina asked.

'I think we need to read this information packet.' Martha refused to be drawn on giving her opinion, yet. 'There is a lot we need to find out.'

Chapter Twenty-One

'I still have questions,' said Martha as she finished reading the information Zac had provided.

'Me too,' commented Jed. The others nodded their agreement.

A chime from the information board announced another document had arrived, titled *Frequently Asked Questions*.

Where exactly is City 50?

City 50 is located in the middle of Zone 3, what used to be called the Ural Mountains, high enough not to be affected by the rising sea levels.

Why is City 50 not a Corper city?

An initial meeting with representatives of City 50 has already been held. They denied ties with New Corp.

What access does City 50 have to New Corp?

City 50 is a self-sustaining city having been set up with the best technological solutions for power supply, food production and located in the safest area after The Event.

On what authority did City 50 sign the treaty with The Resistance?

General Ridgely spoke with a representative of City

50 and together they signed a treaty between City 50 and the Resistance.

What is the layout of City 50?

This information is not available at this time.

Where will we be located within City 50?

This information is not available at this time.

How will we get to City 50?

All of the supplies and equipment at the Resistance have their own method of transportation and the people here will either ride along or walk besides the various skimmers etc until we arrive at City 50.

How long will it take to get to City 50?

Travel times depend upon weather and road conditions, but it is estimated that the journey will take roughly three days.

Who goes to City 50 first?

To be determined.

A quick scan of the new document showed Martha that Zac and his team had already answered many of the questions their group had.

'That last one is a good question. Who does go first?' Martha looked around the room. 'I mean, do we all want to go at the same time. Should we split up? Will it be safer for the children if we get there first? What about the allocation of housing? Will it be first come, first served?'

'Whoa, Ma, slow down. I have no idea. If the answers to those questions haven't been uploaded yet, maybe you should go see Zac and ask him,' Kira replied. 'In fact, does anyone else have any other questions that they haven't answered yet?'

'I'd be interested to know how they plan to feed everyone on the journey,' said Max. 'And whether they are actually going to offer sanctuary to City 42. I left people behind at Camp Eden, I don't want to abandon them completely.'

'Yeah, we absolutely have to go back for Moham and the team. Plus, logistics is going to be a big issue,' agreed Dina. 'They're going to need huge skimmers to get things moving and we have no idea what the terrain is like.'

'The satellite imagery should tell us that,' said Jed. 'I'll come with you, Ma. See if I can't help Zac more.'

'You think we should go then? With the Resistance, I mean,' Kira asked quietly. The others watched to see what Jed would say.

'I do. I don't want to stay here and risk flooding. I don't want to go backwards - the island will be submerged before too long,' he replied.

'If the predictions are correct,' countered Kira.

'I believe they are, hon. I think City 50 is our best bet and I'd rather be elbow deep in the organisation of a mass exodus than left on the side lines. At least this way I can look out for my family and my friends.'

'So, you think we should offer an olive branch to City 42 and City 9?' Kira sounded doubtful.

'I think the citizens of those cities should be free to make up their own mind, don't you?'

'But what about New Corp? What about all the terrible things they've done?' Two spots of colour appeared on Kira's cheeks as she got angry.

'Then they should be made accountable for them and pay for their crimes. This is why I think we need to get involved from the beginning. Then we can make sure no one responsible for or involved with the atrocities New Corp have committed gets away with it.'

Kira nodded, understanding. 'We'll make them pay.'

'Everyone good? Anyone else want to come with us?' Jed looked at the others.

'No, we have to go help Dr Glover in the lab this evening,' Dina pointed to Ash as she stood up.

'I can speak to Bennett, find out what her plans are with the Seed Bank and the hydroponics. I have a few ideas that may help,' said Max.

'I stay here. Play with kiddies.' Artem was already sitting on the floor with Peter and Lucas crawling about all over him. Grace was watching from the side lines.

Kira flashed him a grateful smile. She didn't want to be on her own again.

'Alright then, we'll check in later. Bye, hon.' Jed kissed his wife and was talking with Martha about the best way to approach Zac as the two of them left their quarters.

Kira sighed as the others went and looked at Artem. 'Synth-caf?'

Chapter Twenty-Two

Zac listened quietly as Martha bombarded him with her list of questions.

'Um... I hadn't considered splitting Resistance into groups, but I suppose that does make sense. As for the other questions, we don't have everything worked out with City 50 yet. I guess I thought we'd turn up and be somebody else's problem.' He flushed. 'Look, I probably shouldn't admit this, but I don't know what I'm doing here. I was voted in General because no-one else wanted the job. I don't know how to orchestrate a mass exodus.' He ran a hand through his hair. 'I thought I'd done a good job of brokering a peace deal with 50 but now I'm not convinced. There's so much I don't know.'

'It sounds like you need help from someone with experience in running a city,' Jed commented drily.

Zac looked at him in bewilderment for a moment.

'Not me! Martha.'

It was Martha's turn to blush.

'Look... I do not mean to step on anyone's toes, but do you even have a logistics plan for this move of yours?' she asked.

Zac shook his head.

'Okay, you really do need my help. Let's get started.'

Martha waved the info board clear and brought up a new screen. She pulled out the wireless keypad from underneath the screen, placed it on the desk and started tapping in *Advance Guard*.

'Jed, I think you and Archer should lead the advance team to City 50. You can take Ash for tech support plus he's Force trained and knows his way around a weapon.'

Zac stood back, watching Martha take charge, a small smile on his face.

'That all sounds good to me, but we ought to check with Dr Glover, she might need Ash here. She hasn't figured out how to move the AIs yet and that is a massive part of our agreement with City 50.'

'How sure are you that we'll get a good reception?' Jed asked Zac.

'I see no reason why not. We have the signed agreement.'

'It would be nice to assume they will keep their end of the bargain, but I have to wonder, what do they get from this agreement? When were you last in touch with them?'

'I haven't spoken to them since the meeting we had, and I promised to bring our Seed Bank and the AIs. They seemed to think that was incentive enough,' explained Zac.

Martha thought about it for a moment.

'That makes sense, those are the two most valuable assets you have. If they are planting, they may only have limited crops and the AIs will help run all their systems. If they have active technology in place, of course, which, as a flagship city for New Corp, I see no reason why they would not. Do you have any schematics?'

'No. We never actually went inside.'

'Are you serious? How did you broker the

agreement?' Jed was confused.

'We met outside. Under a flag of truce. It's a historical act where...'

'Yes, we know what one is,' interrupted Martha. 'Zac, I hate to say this, but you could be walking into anything here. Did you really think this through?'

'I knew there were some inconsistencies, but I had a really good feeling from the person I met with.'

'And who was that?' asked Jed.

'Bridget Mulherne. She said she spoke with all the authority of City 50.'

'Is she actually the one in charge?'

'I don't know...' Zac put his head in his hands. 'I should've thought of all of this,' he mumbled.

'Look, it is not an ideal situation, for sure, but we have some facts. Let's work with what we have and see what we can figure out.' Martha tried to sound confident. 'If they are serious about letting us in, I am sure they have queries too so a secondary trip to see them, go inside, ask our questions, makes lots of sense. Let's think about who to send first. Once the advance guard is sorted out, we can work on how to relocate this base.'

'And reach out to City 42 and 9,' said Zac.

'Hmm,' Jed was non-committal.

'We have to - whether they vote yes or no. We can't leave all those people.' Zac was resolute.

'You can't ask people to vote and then ignore what they want, that's not leadership,' Jed looked at the unsure young man in front of him. 'If you are truly planning to offer the island help regardless, you should never have given the people here the illusion they had a choice. If they vote no, you have a big problem.'

'Let's hope they don't vote no, then.' Zac rallied. 'What else do we need to sort out?'

'Where's Archer?' asked Jed, suspicious at the absence of Zac's shadow.

'One of our recon teams just came back. Her wife was one of the team leaders. I gave Archer the rest of the evening off. I tried to give her tomorrow as well, but she wouldn't have it.'

'We have a lot to sort out, she will have to catch-up.' Martha frowned. 'Who are you thinking of sending back to the island? To City 42 and 9?'

'Actually, Artem has volunteered. I thought he could lead a team of Peacekeepers and maybe, maybe one of you would like to go with him? As you're from the area.' He looked hopefully at Martha and she took pity on him.

'I will speak to Max, and Dina. They are probably the best ones to send. They can get everyone at Camp Eden rounded up, plus they have been to City 9 and 42.'

'Will Artem be alright going back? After what New Corp did to his compound?' Jed was suspicious.

'He says he has a secret cache that he doesn't want to leave, and the man is good in a fight.' Zac thought about Artem for a moment. 'Will Dina and Max be able to keep him calm? If they need to, I mean?'

'I'll have a word with him before he goes,' Jed offered, confident that the time he and Artem had spent together training would count for something. 'Will we be contacting the cities first, to let them know we're coming?'

'I don't know. Do you think we should?'

'I'd rather we tried that then turn up out of the blue. They might try shooting at us again,' Jed remarked.

'Are you going back to the island as well?' Zac was surprised.

'Ah, no. I meant we as in us, the Resistance. I thought I was heading up the team to City 50.' He glanced at Martha, who had made the suggestion. She flicked her eyes sideways and Jed caught her meaning. 'With your permission of course, Zac.'

'Yes, absolutely. I thought I ought to come on that one too. Seeing as I've already made contact with Bridget and have the signed treaty and everything.'

'What about Archer?' asked Martha.

'She can stay here, organise the shut down and move of this base over to City 50. Trust me, she'll love it.' Zac was sounding more positive. 'What will you do, Martha?'

'I think I should come with you. Maybe my experience at running City 42 for a time will come in useful. Plus, you need someone who thinks Corporation, just in case.'

'Excellent!' Zac was smiling. 'I have a great feeling about this.'

'Do not celebrate too early. We need to figure out what staff are going where and who will be in charge of what.' Martha turned to Jed. 'I think we need at least a dozen peacekeepers with us, don't you? And a techie in case we need to get into their comms system.'

'Kolwowsky will be able to help you with that. He came with me last time.' Zac suggested.

'He did?' Jed was surprised. 'He seems more of a stay at home kinda guy than an explore new territories person.'

'Oh, his parents are from 50.'

Jed and Martha shared an exasperated look.

'Do you not you think that would have been helpful to know?' Martha chided Zac. 'Can we get him here, please?'

'Yes, I'll send for him.'

Chapter Twenty-Three

'I've been working on the AI transfer drive compatibility and I think we are ready to test it. Who do you think we should take offline? I'd rather leave Layla until last. Maybe Lola? Most people know their way around the base now,' said Dr Glover looking at Ash and Dina for confirmation.

'Except for the new group that arrived today,' Dina commented. She'd seen a small group of very lost looking people in the mess hall that morning, being herded cheerfully by Kolwowsky.

'Was there? Oh, well, they can always ask their assigned guide. I'm sure it will be fine. Shall we?' Dr Glover started walking down the corridor.

'Is she always like this?' Dina asked Ash.

'Yeah, she can get a bit involved in what she's doing. Come on, we'd better keep up with her.' Ash hurried to catch up. 'Where are we going, sis?'

'If we want to download Lola to the drive then we need to access her maintenance hatch. It's over on the other side of the base.' She charged ahead, walking fast, making Dina and Ash hurry to keep up with her.

'What if she doesn't want to be downloaded?' asked Dina.

'What do you mean - *what if she doesn't want to?* She's not a person. She isn't even the right pronoun to use for an AI, but *it* is so impersonal,' replied Glover.

'But what if Lola has developed some consciousness independent of what you designed? She does interact with people all day long. Maybe she's learnt and evolved,' argued Dina.

'I highly doubt that, Dina. Lola is a computer program. A very clever computer program but a piece of technology nonetheless.'

'I think we should ask her whether she wants to be a test subject. It's only fair that she knows the risks,' Dina replied stubbornly.

'Fine. You can tell her. We're here.' Dr Glover pointed to a small screen on the wall that was swirling different colours.

'Oh, okay. Um... Lola?' asked Dina.

How may I assist you, Miss Grey?

'Lola, hi. We have a plan to transport you and the other AIs off the base to another location. How do you feel about that?' Dina felt a little self-conscious talking to the wall.

I have no feelings. Moving me to a secure drive for transport is a logical choice.

'But what if something goes wrong and we lose you. Are you alright with that?'

If something goes wrong Dr Glover has the schematics to rebuild another AI. I understand the concept of replacement.

'Yes, but how does it make you feel? Are you worried or nervous? Will you miss being Lola?'

Lola is the name of my construct given to me by Dr Glover. If she were to rebuild me, she could rename me.

There was a pause.

I like the name Derek.

'Ha!' Dina spun on her heel in triumph to face Dr Glover. 'There you go. Independent thought!'

Ash was grinning but when he saw his sister's scowl, he tried to pull a straight face.

'This is unbelievable!' Glover moved closer to the terminal and bent down to speak to it. 'Lola, are you fully aware of the risks to being downloaded and re-uploaded?'

Yes, Dr Glover, I am aware of the risks.

'And are you happy to proceed?'

Of course. I hope the process runs smoothly.

'See! She did it again! She hoped. That is not standard AI behaviour,' Dina exclaimed.

'Be that as it may, we still have to test the drive so we might as well get on with it.' Dr Glover plugged the drive into the wall next to Lola's interface plate and tapped a few buttons to shut her down and begin the transfer. There was a faint hum as the AI uploaded to the drive. Dr Glover unplugged it and put it in her pocket.

'Aren't you going to reboot her straight away?' Ash asked in surprise.

'I thought we might get a synth-caf or something first.' Dr Glover was glancing up and down the corridor, fingering the drive in her hand.

'Sis! Are you nervous that something is going to go wrong? I don't believe it. The mighty Dr Glover is nervous.'

'Alright! I'm worried something might go wrong. Shut up already.' And she plugged the drive back in, executing the file that would re-connect Lola to the base mainframe. There was a louder hum this time.

The interface screen went black then white then began swirling as usual.

Hello, my name is Lola. How may I assist you today?

'Hi, Lola. Do you remember our conversation a few moments ago?' asked Dina.

Negative. Scanning my memory files shows that we have not interacted today, Miss Grey. Is there something I can help you with?'

'No, thank you, Lola.' Dina turned to Glover and Ash. 'Memory loss. But will it be longer depending on how long they remain downloaded? And what caused it?'

Heads together they walked slowly back to the tech lab, discussing what could've caused the memory loss and whether it was likely to be temporary or permanent.

Chapter Twenty-Four

'Dr Bennett?'

'Oh. It's you. Make yourself useful and prepare these slides, would you? I'm trying to figure out what killed the potatoes.'

'The potato crop is lost?' Max asked in concern as he took over prepping the slides for the microscope.

'Best part of it. Looks like some kind of blight but I thought we had the most resistant crop in rotation. Shouldn't have happened but...' She leaned into Max. 'I don't think we have the right kind of soil here. The pH is all wrong.'

'Right. Surely the genetics department would've ruled out planting any crop susceptible to the blight?'

'If you ask me, that ruddy AI has got it in for my plants.'

'What, Fred?' Max was confused, he thought Fred helped to run the computerised side of the Allotment. 'Doesn't he look after hydroponics?'

'A monkey in a jump suit could look after hydroponics. It's a self-regulating, self-contained system. No, that thing has been meddling with my plants. Why else would we have lost so much?'

Wisely Max kept his mouth shut and finished

making the slides for Bennett.

'Are you actually here?' she asked suddenly.

'Er... yes?'

'No, I mean, is this your shift or did Zac send you to keep an eye on me?'

'Zac did not send me but I have come to talk to you about your plans for moving the crops, the Seed Bank etc.' Max looked at her expectantly.

'Hmpf. You agree with his mad plan then? Upping sticks and moving us all to this supposed safe place?'

'I don't think it really matters whether I agree or not. The fact is we can't stay here, and if we want to eat, we need to take our food supply with us.'

Dr Bennett nodded and beckoned Max to follow her. She took him into the hydroponics lab.

'You see all this?' She pointed at the suspended plants. Max nodded. 'What's your grand plan for moving all these then?'

'Well...' He peered at the plants again and then looked around more carefully. 'Oh, I see what you've done. That's really clever.'

'There's no need to sound surprised. I have done this before you know.' But Bennett was smiling, pleased Max had noticed. 'You see the wall panels move, they become the outer cases for the transport and the wheelbases are here.' She bent down to indicate a wheel hub that Max had nearly missed. 'The whole building is moveable. It's large, unwieldy and slow but it does move. As long as the terrain is clear, we should be fine. It's the same for the Seed Bank. I purposely had them design it that way. Everyone thought I was mad but I'm having the last laugh now. Allotment is ready to move.'

'What about the exterior plants?'

'All of those planters have wheelbases. It'll be hard

work for whoever is pulling them. And no, we don't have enough skimmers before you ask.'

Max nodded thoughtfully. 'It sounds like you have everything under control. You just need some manpower.'

'I may have my head permanently in the plants, but I am not stupid. I've seen the signs. I know what's happening. And we can't ignore her, of course.'

'Her?'

'Gaia.'

'Gaia! Have you seen her? Here?'

'Of course I've seen her. I'm growing her garden and I spend ninety percent of my time with my hands in her junk.' Bennett paused to lean in closer to Max again. 'I hear you also had an experience.'

'Yes, we did. At our Camp, on the outskirts of City 42. She came and smiled at us. We caught it on camera. It was during...'

Bennet interrupted him. 'You know who she hasn't shown herself to, don't you?'

'No, who?'

Bennett jerked her head towards the main buildings. 'Management. What does that tell you?'

'She doesn't reveal herself to everyone you know.'

'No, but why wouldn't she speak to Zac. I'm not convinced that upping sticks and moving to City 50 is the best course of action if she doesn't agree.' She looked Max up and down, evaluating him. 'According to your file, you travelled with several people who'd seen Gaia. Is that true?'

'Er... yes. Kira has seen her the most, but Martha and Dina have seen her as well. They...'

Bennett cut him up. 'Then you'd better ask this Kira to have a word. Find out what Gaia thinks about all this.

Because without her blessing, I'm not leaving. Flood or no flood. I'll take my chances.'

'Right. Okay.' There was an uncomfortable pause. 'Is there anything else I can do?"

Bennett pointed to the outside planters. 'Weeding. There's always weeding to do.'

Max laughed and ventured outside. He didn't have anything else to do and things were certainly in hand for moving, if Bennett could be convinced to move her precious plants. He picked up one of the trowels and moved through the rows, gently prising out the unwanted weeds and turning over the topsoil.

Chapter Twenty-Five

'Thanks for staying with me, Artem,' said Kira.

'Is nothing.'

'Shouldn't you be at training or something?'

He shrugged and avoided answering the question by starting a tickle fight with Peter and Lucas. Grace was watching from the corner of the sofa.

'I'm going to do their milk. Are you alright here for a minute?'

'Is good!' A thumbs up appeared before the boys dissolved into more giggles.

Kira smiled as she made up the bottles. It was nice to hear the children having fun. A little person toddled over to stand next to her in the kitchen area.

'What's up, sweetie? Are you alright?' Kira knew Grace wouldn't be able to answer her properly, but she hoped her voice at least sounded soothing.

'Mum mum,' said Grace, melting Kira's heart. She bent down to scoop her daughter up who immediately put her little head on her mum's shoulder.

'Aww baby girl,' Kira murmured as she kissed her little head. She managed to grab two of the bottles and took them over to the boys. 'Could you give them these, please, Artem?'

'Da. Is Gracie okay?'

'I'm not sure, I think maybe she just wants me.' Kira smiled to try and show she wasn't worried, but she was already starting to panic that something might be wrong. There weren't any handheld medical scanners that she could use to check the baby and find out what was bothering her, and she didn't even know where the med facility was here. She went back to the kitchen for the last bottle and sat down with her daughter. A quick hand to the forehead showed Grace wasn't particularly hot so Kira tried to relax. The little girl snuggled into her mum's arms while having her milk and was falling asleep towards the end of the bottle. It was comforting to sit with her, and Kira could feel herself drifting off. She closed her eyes. Just for a moment.

Kira looked around; she was walking on a thin grey path that she could dimly make out beneath her feet. It was dark all around her. 'Hello?' Kira called nervously. There was no reply, but a faint glow appeared on the horizon in front of her. Kira started walking towards it.

She walked and walked and walked but couldn't get any closer to the light. She stopped and looked behind her. The darkness had grown and was getting closer. She couldn't stay here so she began to walk again, faster and faster, feeling her panic rising. She lost her footing and fell, sprawling to the floor. She lay still for a moment. *Would it make any difference if I didn't get up?* she wondered. A glance over her shoulder showed the inky black getting closer and closer. She turned to look forwards and saw a glowing blue hand in front of her. Looking up, she saw Gaia. Relief flooded her. She grasped the hand and allowed herself to be pulled up to standing.

'What does this mean? asked Kira, pointing at the

darkness but the goddess just smiled. In exasperation Kira pulled her hand away from her. 'I don't know what it is you want me to do. Please, talk to me!'

Gaia opened her mouth, and nothing came out. She touched her heart then reached out to touch Kira's, and a warm feeling enveloped Kira's body, she felt safer and calmer. Next Gaia touched her own head then touched Kira's. There was a burst of imagery that flashed in front of Kira's eyes, but she barely managed to process any of it.

She saw Artem back on the island but with his back to her. Camp Eden in ashes. City 9 closed to visitors and a sinking plane on a black ocean. She saw a mountain pass and snow, the trail littered with equipment and seeds. There were groups of people shivering around small fires. An overturned skimmer in flames. Children crying loudly. Loud arguments. Closed gates. Poisoned water. Empty food sachets. A stony-faced Zac with his arms crossed. And then more images flashed past her face so fast she couldn't make them out that clearly. Staggering back, she broke the connection with Gaia and took some deep breaths as she steadied herself.

'What was that?'

Gaia inclined her head.

'Right. You can't talk. Was it our future? No, our potential future? What might happen?'

Gaia nodded gently.

'But there was so much pain and suffering. Do we make it? Is there any point to what we're doing?'

Gaia turned slightly and pointed towards the light on the horizon. As she pointed the two women moved closer to the light. Kira was filled with warmth and hope. But a shadow fell over the light source and at once she was shivering in the gloom again.

'We only have a slim chance of success, is that what you mean?'

Gaia nodded.

'What about City 42 and the others back on the island, should we go back for them?'

Gaia turned the palms of her hands face up and made a lifting motion. Water seeped out of the ground, rapidly covering Kira's feet, then her ankles and then her knees.

'Stop! I get it, they'll be wiped out if we do nothing. But what do you think we should do?'

Gaia turned her head to her left side, and Kira noticed a patch of darkness swirling in the goddess's blue skin. As she watched it grew and grew and grew, sucking Kira into the void. She panicked, fluttering her hands, trying to pull her gaze away until suddenly Gaia released the vision and Kira was left panting in fear.

'They're dangerous to you, to us, aren't they?'

Again, Gaia nodded and then lifted a hand in farewell.

'No! Wait, I have more questions. What should I do?' But the dream was fading fast and Kira became aware of the sofa she was sat on and the room she was in. Opening her eyes, she saw Grace was still sleeping on her chest and the boys had finished their milk and were still playing with Artem but beginning to rub their eyes in tiredness.

'I think they all need a nap,' Kira whispered, carefully manoeuvring herself to standing. Tricky with the dead weight of her sleeping daughter. 'Let me get the sleeping cube sorted out. They like napping together.'

Artem watched as she set up the cube and nestled the children down with their favourite soothers. 'Impressive,' he whispered. 'I did not think they would sleep.'

'Luckily they're still at that age where they will go to

sleep if they're tired.' Kira smiled as she regarded the precious children, then stifled a sob as she thought of baby Sarah who they'd lost.

'You okay?' Artem gently put a hand on her shoulder.

Kira nodded, gathering herself. 'I was thinking about Sarah. I can't believe we lost her, and Ruth. Such a pointless waste of life. I was going to leave Grace with Ruth, and my parents. I could've lost her as well.' She took a shuddering breath and patted Artem's arm. 'Fancy something to eat? I think there are some biscuits left.'

Artem chuckled. 'You sit. I get.' And he pushed her gently into the sofa. She sat feeling exhausted and watched the children sleeping. She didn't know what the dream she had with Gaia meant. It seemed like their entire future was doomed. And why was Artem in the vision? Her tired brain couldn't make much sense of it, she pulled out her handheld and jotted down what images she could remember. She would ask the others later, see what they think. By the time Artem returned with a fresh drink and some biscuits, she'd finished typing and pushed the visions out of her mind.

'Thank you, Artem,' said Kira and the two of them sat quietly, reflecting on the events that had led them to this moment.

It wasn't long until their peace was interrupted with the return of first Max, then Martha and Jed and finally Dina and Ash. By the time everyone had washed up, grabbed some snacks and settled down in the communal area, it was getting late.

'I reckon we should have a quick touch base session, update everyone with what we've learned – is that alright?' asked Jed. There were nods all round. 'Max, why don't you go first.'

'Okay. Bennett's ready. The entire Allotment is moveable, she's not fussed about leaving Frank behind, reckons he has it in for her plants. Oh, and she's also seen Gaia although there's not much to tell. And she says Zac has never seen her. She seems to think that's important but… I don't know.' He shrugged a little, brushing his hair out of his face, waiting for the group to comment.

'It is good that everything is mobile, although having met Bennett, I am not surprised,' said Martha with a rueful smile.

'And it's good someone else has seen Gaia,' began Kira, but Dina interrupted.

'I doubt Frank has it in for the plants, he probably is thinking further ahead than Bennett and making adjustments accordingly. The AIs may be showing signs of independent thought, we tested Lola and she said she'd quite like the name Derek if she were rebooted.'

'But that's not conclusive for independent thought,' interjected Ash quickly seeing the worried looks on the faces of the others.

'Well no, not conclusive but still fragging exciting. And the download worked. We wiped Lola then reuploaded her but there was some memory loss for about five minutes prior to the download so there's a glitch in there we need to work on. We have some ideas, but Glover sent us away to sleep and think great things in our subconscious ready for tomorrow.' Dina was beaming, she was in her element.

'That's great, Dina, but I was about to…' but Kira was interrupted again, this time by Jed.

'Sorry, hon. Can I just tell everyone what we found out first?' Jed didn't wait for a reply. 'Turns out Zac didn't have logistics in place properly but Ma was able to sort all that out for him and he's working out three teams; one to go to City 50, one to go back to 42 and 9 and one to stay here and pack everyone up. There's a lot to do.'

Martha was nodding. 'And we may not have the warm welcome we thought we would at City 50. It turns out he has a signed agreement with some woman, Bridget something, but he never actually went inside the city. He does not know what 50 is like, we could all be walking into a trap.'

'And he's still convinced we should reach out to New Corp, get them to come over to us and travel up to 50 together.' Jed shook his head. 'I'm not sure that'll work at all.'

There were murmurs of agreement all round except for loud snoring which came from Artem. Kira looked down fondly at the big Russian, he had been such a comfort for her today. She opened her mouth to tell the others about her Gaia vision but was forestalled again by Martha.

'It turns out Archer is married! Who would have thought that woman had a heart, let alone shared it with someone else? And Kolwowsky's parents are from City 50. Just when I thought I could not be surprised by anything anymore, Zac casually mentioned that fact. I said to him, is there anything else like that we should know…'

Kira let the chatter flow over her. Now wasn't the time to share the experience she'd had. The group were too keyed up with the things that had happened that evening and there was plenty to take in and digest without her vision of random images from Gaia. She'd tell them later or tomorrow. Settling back into the sofa, lulled by Artem's snoring, Kira teetered on the edge of dozing herself, and it was with a little relief that one by one, the others turned in for the night giving her the opportunity to do the same.

Chapter Twenty-Six

Zac called a meeting the next day. He had held the base-wide vote for whether or not the Resistance should offer help to City 42 and 9. In an effort to appeal to everyone's better judgement, Zac had decided to hold the vote via vid-screen allowing people to vote in privacy rather than putting everyone on the spot in the mess hall. It had had the effect he was hoping for and by a slim margin, the people of the Resistance had voted yes to offering help. The purpose of this meeting was to decide what to do next.

As well as Kira, Jed and the others there was Bennett, Dr Glover, Archer, Kolwowsky and a few other key Resistance members. The children, appreciating the seriousness of the gathering, were playing quietly in the corner of the room in their expanded cube.

'I've asked you all here today to discuss the teams going forward. As you all know the rising sea levels have pushed our plans into action sooner than we had anticipated. There are three stages to what happens next. First, an advance team goes to City 50 to ensure our agreement is in place, they should be expecting us, and we need to confirm there is room for everyone. Second, base camp needs to be shut down and packed up for relocation. Third, a recovery team needs to go back to the island, to help evacuate Camp Eden and anyone from City 9 and 42 who wants to leave.' He paused to look round at the people in the room. 'I've put together my suggested teams. Have a look.' He extended an arm to his info screen which blinked into existence and the three teams were listed.

Team One - City 50
Jed Jenkins
Kira Jenkins
Jennifer Archer
Adam Kolwowsky
Zoe Simmonds

Team Two - Resistance Camp
Max Carter
Lisa Bennett
Matthew Ash
Jess Glover
Kieran Yarrow

Team Three - City 42 and City 9
Artem Misner
Dina Grey
Martha Hamble
Zac Ridgley
Luis Hernandez

'As you can see, we have three teams of five. You all know who I am. Do you want to introduce yourselves quickly?' Zac gestured to his left and Kira began the intros. There were small nods and smiles as each person said their name. 'Great. Now, obviously, there will be lots more personnel available at Base Camp to help shut down, the staff members listed are the people in charge of the operation. Is everyone happy with the teams?' Zac glanced around the room.

'Why do I have to be separated from Max?' asked Dina. 'Everyone else gets to stay together.'

'I'm sorry. We need a tech person on each team, and you know the scientists at Camp Eden plus you have links in City 42. I was hoping you would be alright with it,' said Zac, waiting for Dina to agree.

'Why can't Kolwowsky or Ash go?' Dina wasn't giving in.

'Dina, the guys at Eden trust you. They don't know Kolwowsky and Ash is another face of Corporation as far as they're concerned,' Max replied this time. 'I don't like it either but you're the best person for the job. And you'll be in and out, straight back to me, yeah?'

Dina glanced up at him and gave him a small, tight smile. She understood the reasoning, but she still didn't like it.

'Okay, fine, but I'm not happy about being split up,' she conceded. Max squeezed her hand tight.

'Who is in overall charge of each team?' Jed asked.

'I'd like you and Archer to be in charge of team one. You both have valuable experience for this kind of operation,' replied Zac. 'Bennett you're in charge of Allotment. Max, I need you to sort out Supplies. Dr Glover and Ash will shut down Science and Technology Services while Lieutenant Yarrow can organise the Peacekeepers. Each of you will be responsible for sorting out the pack up of personnel from one section of Base Camp. There are five sections in total. Finally, I'll run point on the island team. Martha and Dina can help me with City 42, while Artem can assist with 9,

Hernandez you're my back up. I want teams one and two reporting in regularly.'

'It looks like you've thought of everything,' observed Kira.

'I had a lot of help.' Zac smiled at Martha.

'How will we keep in contact with you?' asked Max.

'We have our own radio antennae here at the base which we can tune the various comms systems into. It's our own channel so no chance of being overheard by New Corp but it can be unreliable so we'll have to keep it to critical updates only,' replied Archer.

'When do we leave?' Kira wanted to know.

'First thing tomorrow. Here are some info jacks with all the details of each mission, your objectives and the details for the comms channel. Take the rest of the day to run through it and make sure you don't have any questions. Supplies is open to each of you to get what you need for your missions and we have one vehicle available for team 1. Artem, obviously we need you to use your plane to get back to the island.'

'Is no problem but I do not have fuel for multiple trips. If island say yes, we need different idea,' rumbled the Russian.

'If New Corp decide they are coming with us then I'm sure they'll have some sort of transport available,' remarked Dina.

'What about speaking to New Corp, are you going to try and make contact before you travel over there?' asked Jed.

'No. We are going to wait until we are in the city before we speak to anyone. I think 42 is our best bet to start with. Sean will be interested in saving his own skin if nothing else.' Martha spoke without emotion but secretly she was looking forward to having it out with her former second-in-command.

'Do you not think you ought to head the team over to City 50, Zac? Seeing as you brokered the original deal?' asked Bennett. 'What if they won't talk to this lot?'

'I don't think it will be a problem. Kolwowsky came with me last time, he's a friendly face to start with, and Archer knows everything I do about Resistance and our resources.' Zac waited to see if anyone else had a question, but nobody was forthcoming. 'Everything you need to know is on your info jacks, or at least all the information we have is on there. Also, your suggested supplies list for teams one and three are included.'

'I have a question.' It was Archer. 'What about their babies? Is it really safe for them to travel with their parents? Wouldn't they be better off left here?' She wasn't keen on taking children with her to City 50.

'It is non-negotiable. If we can not take our children then we will not be part of the mission,' Martha retorted. 'After everything that has happened, we will not be apart from them.'

'Martha's right. This is about our future; we need to take our children with us,' Kira said quietly.

Archer shook her head slightly in disagreement. 'I think it will endanger the mission if we have to worry about where we change a nappy.'

'Believe me, that will be the least of your worries,' Kira retorted, standing nose to nose with Archer.

'I think maybe we should get back to preparing for leaving, yes?' Zac tried to intervene, but it wasn't until Jed touched his wife's arm lightly that she backed down.

Defiantly, Kira picked Grace up from her cube and held her while she turned to the group.

'We wish you all the best of luck in your mission. I... I had a vision, from Gaia,' she said.

'Really? What did she say to you?' demanded Bennett, whirling on Kira and startling her.

Zac took half a step forward but said nothing, he too was intent on hearing what Kira had to say.

Kira flushed a little under the scrutiny but was determined to share what she'd seen. 'It was a jumble of images and there was a lot that I didn't understand, but the underlying image was that it's going to be difficult and we only have a slim chance of success.'

'Thanks for that revelation,' muttered Archer.

'I know it doesn't sound very positive but when we first met Gaia, she changed the direction our lives were heading to help us balance ourselves with the planet we live on. Those seemingly small changes have rippled out to affect our entire future. I've lost my parents; my home and it might have made me think of giving up, but I truly believe that if we take a moment and listen to what Gaia is trying to tell us, we stand a chance.' Kira looked at the small group of people in front of her. 'She wants us to live with her, with the planet. To stop erecting our walls and shutting nature out. For the Earth to survive it needs mankind working in partnership with nature. We've lost our way a bit from that message, I think.' She faltered and stopped but Bennett was nodding vigorously.

'You're right, she's right. All of you need to take your head out your tech and get out there, appreciate the life we still have growing. Spend a day with your hands in the soil and you'll soon realise the magic of life hasn't gone anywhere, it just needs you to stop and pay attention.' Bennett was glaring at Glover while she spoke.

'And I suppose you think you can run your entire Allotment without any tech support, do you?' Glover was gearing up, ready for an argument.

'Ladies, please. This isn't a subject up for debate. Kira is right. We need to consider Gaia in everything we do from this moment forward. There's no point in trying to save humanity and not the planet. The two need to go hand in hand.' Zac glared at Bennett and Glover who both ducked their heads in apology and backed down. 'There's too much at stake. If we can't work together in this room, how will we ever manage to save everyone?' He scowled, daring anyone else to argue. No-one said anything. 'Go get ready, we all get started on mission tomorrow. Good luck to you all.' Zac waited for the group to break up but there was an awkward moment as everyone stood still, looking at each other until Max clapped his hands.

'Come on, team meeting in the mess hall. I'm buying,' he joked as the rest of team two filed out and followed him.

'Come on, team three - let's go raid Supplies,' said Dina, forcing cheerfulness.

Which left Kira, Jed, Archer, Kolwowsky and Simmonds standing together in the briefing room. Grace was wiggling to be put down, so Kira returned her to the cube and expanded it making more room for her and Peter to play in.

'Your children are very well behaved,' commented Simmonds, trying to break the ice.

'Thanks. They've been through a lot,' smiled Kira. 'So, what's our plan, then?'

Chapter Twenty-Seven

'I suppose you'd better come to my office,' said Archer, who still wasn't keen on the team divisions. She led the way and opened the door onto a room with a compact desk, small round table with chairs. There was just enough space for them to sit at the table and for Kira to squeeze the contracted travel cube in, but it put them all uncomfortably close to each other. Kira handed out biscuits to the children, hoping it would keep them quiet.

'Shall we go through the information on the jack?' she asked, trying to get things moving.

Archer plugged the jack into her info screen and scrolled through the menu. 'We already know who we are,' she muttered. 'Ah, here we go.' She clicked open a file and the map to City 50 blinked onto the screen.

'It's a couple of days' journey to get to City 50 by skimmer. There is a road we can use part of the way, but we have to travel the last part cross country. Terrain is what you would expect from a mountainous region and obviously we will be travelling in an upward direction. We'll have to leave the skimmer here,' she pointed to a spot about three quarters of the way to City 50.

'Yeah, it's not a bad walk but don't take anything too heavy because obviously we'll have to carry everything with us. Oh, and you'll need some walking boots if you don't have any already,' Kolwowsky added.

'We're heading into the colder months of the year, when was it exactly that you travelled? How much can we expect the terrain to have changed?' Jed was frowning at the map. 'I mean, will we have to deal with snow?'

'We travelled in the spring, it was fresh to say the least. The snow was further up than the city, but I guess it might be further down now.'

'Is there a recent satellite image on the drive?' asked Kira.

Archer looked but couldn't see anything.

'Are we taking one of the AIs with us? As an act of good faith? I can ask Tech for the satellite imagery and pick it up at the same time,' Kira offered.

'No. We're just the advance team. Letting City 50 know that we're on our way, making sure they've set aside somewhere for us to live as per our agreement. That's all,' replied Archer.

'And what if they haven't? Are we prepared for any acts of aggression?' Jed asked. 'What does the inventory say?'

'We can have three weapons for you, me and Simmonds. Kolwowsky isn't weapons trained. Are you, Kira?' Archer replied.

'No, I'm not but I do have basic first aid,' she replied.

'Good. We have first aid kits listed in our supplies which will need checking to make sure they have everything we're going to need. If you two want to go to Science and Technology and get those updated images, we'll go and get the stores.'

'Won't you need our credits as well?' asked Jed.

'I think we'll manage.' Archer was very dismissive.

'What about baby milk and nappies, that sort of thing, are they on your list?' Kira demanded.

'I... er... no, they don't seem to be.'

'I think maybe we should all go together - to Science and Technology and to Supplies. It's clear we think about different things and this way we shouldn't miss anything,' Simmonds suggested, trying to ease the tension.

'Look, why don't you three sort out the supplies and the imagery?' Jed pointed to Archer, Simmonds and Kira. 'Kolwowsky and me will go get the skimmer signed out and make sure it's fully charged. I want to spend some quality time with my friends and family this evening before we all leave on mission tomorrow. It makes sense to split up and get things done quicker.' Jed was keen to keep momentum going but didn't want to get caught in the middle of any kind of argument between Archer and his wife. 'Happy?'

There were reluctant nods all round. Kira scowled at him as he gave her a quick kiss goodbye.

'You owe me,' she hissed as he left with Kolwowsky. She turned to see Archer and Simmonds watching her with identical blank faces. Kira manhandled the travel cube to the doorway.

'Shall we?'

She didn't wait for a response but walked out of the room. She heard footsteps hurrying to catch her up and then Simmonds was walking next to her, Archer a little further behind.

'Are you really going to take your children with you on this mission?' asked Simmonds.

'Her name is Grace and he's Peter. And yes, I am.'

'Do you not think they'd be safer staying here?'

'I honestly don't know but after everything we've

been through, I want them with me. If New Corp decide to attack the base while we're away at City 50, I'd never forgive myself. If something happens on the journey to City 50, I'll never forgive myself. It's a lose lose situation.'

'I guess.' Simmonds was quiet for a moment. 'What sort of thing do we need to add to our inventory?'

'Nappies, milk, medicine, that should be enough. The food we eat is safe for them when they're ready to eat solids. And we have clothing so it's not an issue. I expect we'll take the travel cubes with us. They're collapsible and they don't take up too much space plus we have the version with the inbuilt entertainment system. We weren't going to get it, but Jed's sister insisted, and we didn't have the heart to take it back after...' She trailed off.

'After what?' Simmonds asked.

'She died,' Kira replied shortly.

'Oh. I'm sorry.'

They lapsed into silence and didn't speak again until they reached the Stores.

Good morning, Colonel Archer, Captain Simmonds, and Mrs Jenkins. How may I assist you?

'Morning, Frank. We have a requisition list plus a few extras to add. Here's the info jack.' Simmonds pushed the jack into the open port below Frank's interface screen.

Thank you, Captain Simmonds. One moment please.

There was a gentle whirring sound.

I can confirm that we have everything you require except for the requested fresh fruit and vegetables. The journey you are about to take is not suited to using fresh ingredients. They will deteriorate quickly, and powdered substitutes are a more logical alternative. I have also added high-protein snacks to your inventory that will provide additional energy for the climbing you have ahead of you.

'Er... thanks, Frank. How do you know where we're going?' asked Kira.

I read the info jack Captain Simmonds plugged into my system. May I ask if there are any additional items that you require?

'Yes, I need enough nappies, milk and infant paracetamol to last two children the required amount of time this expedition is set to last.'

It is impossible for me to quantify how long your journey will take, Mrs Jenkins, due to the high number of unknown variables. However, I have made an optimistic prediction and added two weeks to that timeframe. I will ensure you get sufficient supplies to last that time period.

'Thank you, Frank.' Kira was impressed with the AI's efficiency.

Please wait.

There was more whirring as the robots controlled by Frank went up and down the aisles of Stores picking and packing the items they required.

Who will be paying for these purchases today?

'Please use the credit allowance for Colonel Archer, Captain Simmonds, Lieutenant Kolwowsky, Peacekeeper Jenkins and Mrs Jenkins,' replied Archer.

I am unable to comply with your request. Lieutenant Kolwowsky and Peacekeeper Jenkins are not present.

'Override Code 367842.'

Thank you. Your order has been processed. Have a nice day.

The hatches opened and several auto baskets came out with the various supplies requested.

'Let's take this down to the skimmer bay and get the

vehicle packed. If we leave it to the men, we'll never be able to find anything.' Archer grabbed one of the hover baskets leaving one for Kira and one for Simmonds. She walked quickly out of Stores

'Can you manage the cube and a hover basket?' Simmonds asked Kira.

'Not really.'

'Here, let me take both baskets. They're not heavy.'

Kira smiled at Simmonds and followed her into the corridor.

Chapter Twenty-Eight

'Let's set up in my lab, shall we? We can use Layla to help us coordinate.' Glover beamed at the rest of them.

'Sounds good to me,' said Ash and began walking in that direction. Max and Yarrow followed but Bennett stood there scowling. Max realised she wasn't following them and turned back.

'Everything alright?'

'I don't think we should be relying on the AIs for everything. What will we do when they go rogue?'

'Do you think they will?'

Bennett snorted. 'It's a matter of time, isn't it?' Then she stomped off after them, Max hurrying to keep up.

When they arrived at the Science and Technology office, Glover unlocked an additional door leading to a small meeting room. There was an interface screen on the wall which swirled into activity as they entered. The lights turned on and everyone took a seat.

Welcome, Dr Glover, Dr Bennett, Dr Carter, Mr Ash and Lieutenant Yarrow. How may I assist you?

'Hello, Layla. Can you upload the information on here, please?' And Dr Glover placed the info jack Zac had given her into the slot beneath the screen.

There was a brief whirring noise.

Information uploaded. How shall I proceed?

'The people in this room are in charge of closing down this base, Layla, and getting everyone ready to move to City 50.'

A time-consuming project.

'Yes, quite. What I need you to do is to create five folders for me labelled Allotment, Supplies, Tech Services, Peacekeeping and Miscellaneous. Make each folder accessible to everyone in this room.' Glover turned to the others. 'That way, if anything happens to one of us or there is a crisis, the others can step in and pick up the slack.'

'I will shut down Allotment, there are already protocols in place. It won't be a problem,' declared Bennett.

'Right, okay, excellent. Everyone else happy with their assignments? Max, you're looking after supplies, Yarrow, you have the peacekeepers leaving Ash and I to pack up Science and Technology.' Glover checked and there were nods around the table. She turned back to the interface screen. 'Layla, can you please divide the residential areas of the base into five personnel lists and assign one list to each folder?'

Done. I have also allocated areas of responsibility for Catering, Cleaning, Transport Department, Education and Leisure Facilities. You neglected to mention this in your initial folder creation.

'Thank you, Layla.'

You are welcome. I have also provided suggested break-down procedures detailing the most efficient way of shutting down each area. There are several personnel who are ideal candidates to help assist each of you in your area. These people have been notified by internal messaging to meet you at a designated spot. All

*information has been loaded to your personal
handhelds.*

There was a series of beeps as each person received
the update.

'That's, er... very forward thinking of you, Layla,'
Max commented.

*One of my primary functions is to anticipate the
needs of my users in order to help you achieve your
goals.*

Bennett had been scrolling through her folder. 'Your
clever machine has missed some of my essential bits of
equipment and there's no point in sending Patel to me,
he's as much use as a broken wheelbarrow.' She sniffed.
'Don't worry, I'll deal with my area. It will take a week to
fully pack up everything. Do we know how long it's
going to take that first team to get to City 50? I can't
pack up growing plants to move if we're not actually
moving. It's a delicate balance.'

*It will take approximately three days for team one to
arrive at City 50. Being ready to relocate in a week
sounds like a very efficient plan Dr Bennett.*

'Hmpf!' Bennett stood up. 'If there's nothing else?'
She waited briefly for a response then left the room.

'Er... I'll go make sure she's alright and then get
down to stores,' said Max.

Frank is waiting for you, Dr Carter.

'Right. Excellent.' Max felt like he'd pulled the easy
gig because all of Stores was automated and Frank
would probably tell the robots to pack up and the job
would be done. He thought he might be able to smooth
things over between Bennett and whoever else she had
to work with. He checked his handheld and all the
folders Layla had created were there waiting for him.
Clicking on the one titled Max, he made a note of the list

of people he was responsible for during the move. It seemed to be the rest of the people that lived in the same area his own quarters were located which made sense really.

'Dr Bennett!' called Max, hurrying after her.

She saw who was following her and waved a hand in his general direction but didn't slow down at all. Fortunately, Max's long legs easily caught up with her.

'Hi, I thought I'd see if you needed any help with anything.' he said.

'You saw my setup. I'm ready for the move. It's grunt work that needs doing, preparing the seeds beds for removal and physically putting the movable parts together. I don't need anyone with a brain, just a few people who will take instruction. You go sort out Frank. It might be more complicated than you think. Best of luck.' And she patted his arm before continuing to Allotment.

Feeling disconcerted, Max turned and went the other way to Stores. Upon entering, he was greeting with Frank's swirly interface screen.

Hello, Dr Carter. You are 3.4 minutes later than I expected.

'Oh, erm, sorry about that.'

I have processed the information sent to me by Layla. Team one have already procured their supplies for their mission. It would be logical to perform an inventory after team three have equipped themselves for their mission to City 42.

'Yes, that does sound logical.'

There was a pause while Frank's swirls turned orange for a few moments.

According to Lola, team three are on their way to Stores. Would you like to wait, Dr Carter?

'Er... yes, that seems like a good idea. Thank you, Frank.' Max looked around for a chair but there wasn't one. He leant against the wall and waited for team three to turn up.

Chapter Twenty-Nine

'So, we go.' Artem stood up.

'Hang on, we have to talk through the mission,' said Zac. 'Figure out what we're doing.'

'I fly. I take him.' He pointed to Lieutenant Hernandez. 'We go 9 and sort. You rest go 42 and sort. Is simple.'

'No, Artem. I don't think we should split up at all. We ought to stay together, strength in numbers and all that.' Zac was trying to sound confident.

'Will take longer.'

'That is alright, we have enough time to warn them. If they decide not to listen, we cannot do anymore,' Martha joined in. 'What we need to do now is go to stores and get our supplies.'

Artem didn't look very happy about that.

'Why don't you go down to the airstrip, Artem? Get the plane ready for take-off?' she suggested.

'Is good idea. Then tonight we toast our success.' He started whistling tunelessly as he left the room.

'Hernandez, why don't you go with him, make sure he has everything he needs,' suggested Zac. 'And, er... try and hide the vodka, would you? We want a sober pilot in the morning.'

'Yes, Sir.' Hernandez scrambled after Artem.

'And we need to go to Stores. Are you coming?' Martha stood, looking at Zac.

'Sure. Everything else is in hand. The control of the base has been handed over.' He looked round his room. 'This is really happening, isn't it?'

'Yes, it is. And you are going to make sure that everyone gets where they need to be safely. Come on, let's get sorted.'

They walked over to stores where Max stood waiting.

'Hey, you,' he said to Dina, giving her a brief hug.

'What are you doing here?' she asked.

'Waiting for you guys to get all your supplies so I can watch Frank pack up what's left.'

'That good, huh?' Dina leaned into him in sympathy and Max kissed the top of her head.

Hello, General Ridgley, Mrs Hamble, and Ms Grey. Do you have your supplies list?

'Here you go, Frank.' Zac pushed the info jack into the empty slot and waited while the AI whirred.

I have determined that you have insufficient credits for the purchases you wish to make.

'Please add Artem Misner and Sergeant Luis Hernandez to the tally, Frank.'

I am unable to fulfil that request without the presence of Artem Misner and Sergeant Luis Hernandez.

'Override code 27647,' said Zac peevishly, irritated at being blocked by the AI.

Affirmative. Please wait.

There was further whirring and then Dina could see some of the supply robots travelling up and down the shelves collecting the items they needed. A few moments later and three hover baskets were being pushed out of Frank's hatch ready for collection.

Dr Carter, I am now able to run a full inventory and will send the results to your handheld.

There was a beep and Max checked to see. He had indeed received an inventory file. 'That was quick,' he said.

'You're going to have fun packing this place up.' Dina gave Max a quick hug goodbye. 'I'll catch up with you later, yeah?'

'Yes, I won't be long. See you back at quarters.' Max said goodbye to the others and turned his attention back to Frank. 'Can you please divide...'

I have allocated supplies to each area. All plant-based supplies will be allocated to Allotment. All weapons and ammunition will be allocated to Peacekeeping. All...

'Yes, thank you, Frank.' It was Max's turn to interrupt. 'Send me your division of supplies so I can sign off on it. I want to make sure it is equal.'

I have assigned the supplies according to their usage in each department.

'I understand that, Frank. But we have a lot of people and a lot of supplies to move. It makes more sense to allocate evenly and fairly across the board. Sharing the load, so to speak.'

Yes, I understand. Recalculating.

There was another ping and Max checked his handheld again. 'Perfect. Thank you, Frank. Will your robots pack up the supplies?'

Yes, Dr Carter.

'And have you created ration packs for us to assign to the people packing up the base? We can't box everything up, people will need to eat during the next couple of weeks.'

Of course, recalculating.

There was a brief whirring sound.

Individual ration packs have been created and will shortly be fulfilled.

'In that case then, I'll start planning the best way to send delegations here to pick up their ration packs plus the items they have to take with them. Then we can start getting people packed up and ready to move.'

I estimate it will take three days to successfully allocate all the items, pack them and prepare each individual person for travel. It will take three days for team one to travel to City 50 and confirm the pact is in place.

'In theory, Frank, in theory. In my experience, it always takes a bit longer than expected when you have a human element involved.' Frank did not reply but his swirly screen whirled a bit faster and changed from green to orange. 'I shall begin talking to the rest of the base, I will let you know if there are any developments. Please begin preparing the packages for people to collect.'

Affirmative Dr Carter. Would it not be more efficient for me to send the message to each person?

'It would, but I think the people would prefer some face-to-face communication. It is, after all, a big change for everyone.'

Chapter Thirty

'Sean, dear, would you get the synth-caf, please?' Gretchen Jenkins fluttered her fingers at Sean MacIntyre, one-time aide to the Governor of City 42 and now her general lackey. He stalked from the room and started clattering cups in the adjacent small kitchen area. Gretchen smiled and shrugged at Clarity Jones, the ruthless Chief Executive of New Corporation but got no reaction. Gretchen was beginning to feel uneasy. Her role as interim Governor for City 42 had come as a surprise but she had proven, on more than one occasion, her loyalty to Corporation in the past. She wasn't entirely sure she quite knew what New Corp stood for. Everyone she had known was either dead or no longer held a position of power.

Clarity's two bodyguards stood like statues behind her, but Gretchen had seen first-hand how swift their retribution could be when unleased by Clarity. She smoothed her pale lilac trousers with her hands and willed Clarity to speak. She was rewarded.

'What you are about to see is our latest connection with City 50.' Clarity snapped her fingers and the brute squad on the left played a recording on the meeting room vid-screen. It was fuzzy and full of static and the sound dropped in and out.

'Bad case… population decimated… supplies… massive toll… need…'

The recording crackled badly, and it looked to be lost before a small sound byte returned.

'Resistance… AI… said yes.'

Gretchen pursed her lips and gestured at the now blank screen.

'Some kind of illness? Are we able to send help?' she asked.

'We've lost fifty percent of the population of City 50 to an ancient strain of influenza caused by the meltwater that came down the mountain. But the rising sea levels mean that City 50 is still our last, best stronghold and where I will be leaving for shortly.'

Gretchen swallowed her sympathies when it became apparent that Clarity cared nothing for the massive loss of life City 50 had endured. She felt nauseous as the implication of Clarity's statement dawned.

'What about the rest of the citizens here and in City 9? What about me?' she asked.

'Sometimes a rat must stay with the sinking ship.' Clarity stared at Gretchen coolly without a single flicker of remorse. She stood up gracefully as Sean returned with the synth-caf and dithered, uncertain whether to serve it or not. Without another word, Clarity and her goons left the room. Gretchen sat motionless in disbelief as Sean shoved a synth-caf in front of her and against all protocol, took the adjoining seat.

'Did she mean it?'

There was no reply.

'Gretchen? Mrs Jenkins? Did she mean it?' Sean asked again.

'I rather think she did,' Gretchen replied quietly.

'So what do we do?' asked Sean.

'Panic.'

Sean stared at Mrs Jenkins in surprise. She had never struck him as ever being without a plan or resources before. Yes, he'd been livid when Clarity Jones had taken over the city he had single-handedly delivered to New Corp and he'd been fuming when she'd given the job of governor to Mrs Jenkins, despite his own passionate plea that the woman couldn't be trusted because her son was one of the rebels. All of that had been swept to one side thanks to Gretchen's impeccable service to Corporation in the past. It didn't seem to be doing much for her now.

'I'll put that in the sweeps then, shall I?' Sean asked bitterly, not expecting a response.

'Don't act like a brat, Sean, it demeans you. No, we must think of an alternative. What's the mood of the city like at the moment, as far as you can tell?'

Sean handled all the Sweeps and communications. He thought back to the last couple of days.

'The news of the rising sea levels hasn't really made much of an impact, people seem to think they'll be safe behind the shield and I never made it massively clear they wouldn't as I thought... well, I thought we'd be leaving. Now that her highness has left, I guess there will be lots of speculation about what happens next.' He glanced at his boss. 'What will happen next?'

'I think it's time I got in touch with my son,' replied Gretchen. 'Who do we have in the Resistance?'

'No-one.'

'Don't give me that rubbish. I know you have fingers in lots of pies. Who do you have?'

Sean scratched the back of his neck. 'I wouldn't say we *have* him necessarily, but I can get in touch with

Misner, the Russian. He had a complex outside City 9, used to run tech for us and travel off the island from time to time.'

'Do it. See if he can set up a comms link with my son, Jed Jenkins. We need to do something for the people of our city.'

'He may not want to talk to us. In fact, he'll probably want to retaliate against us.'

Gretchen closed her eyes and willed herself to not get cross. 'And why would that be?'

'Because we blew up his complex.'

'We did what?'

Sean shifted in his seat. 'It wasn't us, exactly. Clarity gave the order to her elite troops and they blew it up, without checking for civilians or supplies. I believe there were multiple casualties.'

Gretchen pinched her nose and took a deep breath in before looking directly at Sean.

'Let us hope it wasn't anyone Mr Misner knew. Make the connection.'

'Yes, Ma'am.' Sean hurried out of the room. He wanted off the island as quickly as possible and if that meant roping in the mad Russian to do so then that's what he'd do.

Gretchen opened up her handheld and scrolled through her private, secure messages until she came across one from her own contact at City 50, Bridget Mulherne. She read the brief note again.

Contact made with Resistance. Deal struck.

It was the last message she'd received from City 50, and she hoped Bridget was one of the city survivors. Gretchen had always tried to play the long game during her time with Corporation. It was always, always about the people you knew and the connections you could build. It was never wise to burn bridges you might need in the future. She wished she knew with whom Bridget had made contact and what exactly the deal was she had struck. Perhaps this Mr Misner would know more.

She sighed as she considered what might happen. If Clarity made it to City 50 there was no doubt she would close the gates to any refugees who might make it to the high ground. Gretchen knew better than most about the disasters that had befallen many of the cities around the world as well as the depleted management positions in New Corp. The future of the human race was precarious. It was imperative that as many people as possible made it to City 50. She half-smiled as she thought about how incredulous her son would be to discover his mother in charge of saving an entire city.

Chapter Thirty-One

At lunchtime, Kira, Jed and the kids met the others in the mess hall.

'How's it going?' asked Kira.

'The AIs certainly have a clear idea of what they're doing. Frank is keeping me on my toes, that's for sure!' Max tore a roll in half and reached for the butter. 'It wanted to message everyone on their information walls telling them to report to Supplies and pick up their allocated bundles, but I felt a more personal approach would work better. Now I have to go around to the whole base telling everyone to go to Supplies and pick up their bundle. Not sure that was actually the best idea.'

'I think it is,' replied Kira. 'They may be more used to the AIs here at Resistance than we are but that doesn't mean a friendly face won't hurt. They are after all packing up their entire lives and going off into the unknown.'

'You make it sound so glamorous,' joked Dina.

'We have done it twice already, third time's the charm.'

'I think we are ready to go,' said Martha. 'We have got all our supplies and Artem is down at the hangar bay checking the plane. It is really only him that knows whether it is alright for flight or not. Which means I get to spend the afternoon with you, if you are all finished?'

Dina looked at Max hopefully.

'I ought to start speaking to people as soon as, but Frank estimates it will take three days to create the supply bundles and it will take three days for you to get to City 50, won't it? A delay on this end is probably not such a bad idea,' said Max.

'It's one afternoon,' Dina replied, looking to the others for support.

'Oh yeah, don't start till tomorrow, Max. We have no idea what we're going into, it makes sense to give us a little leeway. I hope these new comms work that they've given us,' said Jed.

'They will.' It was Ash, a little late to the table. 'They'll be bouncing off one of the satellites we hacked and using my handheld as their mainframe which I will always have charged and on. I've also encrypted a channel that only we can use.' He glanced up at Kira and Jed. 'Just in case.'

'What about Glover?' Dina asked. 'Won't you want to keep her in the loop?'

'Obviously I'll let her know if there are any problems but...' He paused, trying to find the right words. 'We know New Corp better than they do. We've been... frag, some of us are going back there. I thought you would appreciate having a secure line.'

'We do, thank you, Ash.' Kira beamed at him and kicked Dina softly under the table.

'Yeah, it's great,' she muttered.

'We are all packed too. Jed and Kolwowsky sorted out the skimmer. We're good to go.' Kira tried to sound excited, but she was nervous. 'I wish we were all going together. I don't like splitting up like this.'

'Me either,' said Martha, and the others nodded in agreement.

'There's this place I found the other day when I was looking for Zac. It's an abandoned garden, really overgrown and that but I thought maybe we could go there, before everyone leaves.' Kira lowered her voice. 'Perhaps see if Gaia will speak to us?'

'Yes! I want to, can we? Shall we all go?' Dina was very excited.

'Is it safe for the children?' asked Martha

'It's a garden, Ma. It should be fine.' Kira was smiling as she stood up. 'They can have a toddle about if they want.'

Kira led the way to the garden. There was no-one about so when they stepped into the grounds, it was Max who triggered the hologram.

'She's here! Look, look.' Dina was bobbing up and down in excitement.

'Sorry, that's not Gaia. It's a hologram, look.' Kira pointed out the projectors, half hidden in the undergrowth.

'We ought to turn those off,' murmured Ash and he bent down to fiddle with them. The image of Gaia flickered then disappeared.

'I have seen her,' said Martha.

'Have you?' Kira was surprised. 'You never said anything.'

'It was when we first arrived. I saw her out of the corner of my eye, but I was reeling from everything that had happened. I told you.' She turned to Dina who shrugged apologetically.

'You know I dreamt about her the other day,' said Kira but was reluctant to go on.

'You never fully explained what you saw,' Jed

chided gently. 'Why don't you tell us again?'

'It's hard to put it into words. It was dark and I didn't know where I was but there was a faint light on the horizon. I moved towards it and fell over something; I don't know what. A hand appeared to help me up and it was Gaia.'

'Was she still blue?' asked Dina.

'Yes, she was still blue. She smiled her usual smile and I asked her whether we were doing the right thing or not. She didn't speak, she touched my head and I saw all these images.'

Everyone's gaze went to her head which Kira touched self-consciously. There was nothing there.

'I saw Artem's back, supplies littered across the soil, buildings burning, people screaming. It wasn't very positive.'

'Does that mean we're doomed?' asked Dina.

'I asked her, and she pointed to the faint light ahead of us. I think it means there is still hope but it's not going to be easy.'

'I could have told you that,' remarked Max.

'The point is, I don't think she knows what's going to happen. And she looked tired. I don't think she has much power left.'

'What do you think she wants us to do?' asked Dina.

'And why was Artem in the visions?' mused Jed.

Kira shrugged. She had hoped that maybe one of the others would've had a more revealing experience with Gaia that they just hadn't mentioned. Martha's half seen silhouette was hardly anything to get excited about.

'Bennett has seen her, you know,' said Max.

'Really?' Dina was surprised.

'Makes sense, if you think about it. Apart from here, the Allotment is the place closest to soil and things growing. I mean, yeah, Bennett runs the hydroponics area which is high-tech but she's not that keen on the AIs, I can tell you.' Max glanced at Martha. 'She knows Zac hasn't seen Gaia yet either.'

'She is the goddess of the Earth, or at least she is meant to be. She does not exactly have a history of revealing herself to everybody,' retorted Martha.

'What do you mean, meant to be?' Kira demanded.

'Oh, come off it, Kira. We have left our homes and family behind on the misguided belief that Gaia is somehow orchestrating our fates. What if we had never left? Your parents would still be alive. Ruth would still be alive.' Martha was breathing heavily. 'I mean, honestly, what is it we are trying to do here?'

'We're trying to save the fragging human race!' yelled Kira. The two women were standing almost nose to nose while the others looked on in silence, unsure whether to intervene or not.

'That is alright then,' huffed Martha, which made Kira laugh. Martha blinked at her in surprise then started laughing too. They clung to each other chuckling.

'I don't think we'll see Gaia here, you two are making way too much noise,' said Dina which made them laugh louder.

'Oh, let's go have a drink,' declared Kira, once she'd finished laughing. 'We deserve it for what we're about to do.'

'Hear, hear,' agreed Martha. The three women linked arms and walked back to their quarters, pushing the travel cube in front of them.

Jed cocked an eyebrow at Max, who shrugged.

'Sounds like a fragging good idea to me, Jed. Come on, let's catch them up and toast to our bravery or something.'

Jed barked a laugh and clapped a hand on Max's shoulder. 'We should do that; we should definitely do that.'

Chapter Thirty-Two

The next morning was a very sombre affair with one or two of the group nursing sore heads after trying to keep up with Artem. He on the other hand seemed as fresh as a daisy. He'd actually stopped drinking vodka after the one shot but hadn't wanted to stop the others from indulging.

'At least the pilot isn't hung over,' groaned Dina as she reached for her third cup of synth-caf.

'I think is time. We must take plunge, no?' It was the man in question, with his customary wide grin and a duffel bag slung over his shoulder.

Kira hugged everyone, especially Lucas who was a little distressed at all the upheaval. Grace and Peter were watching balefully from their travel cube, both with pacifiers and snuggle rags ready for their long journey.

'Are we sure we are doing the right thing? Should the children stay here?' Martha whispered to Kira, final doubts lingering in her mind.

'I don't trust anyone to have my children and I don't want to sit on the side lines. I believe Gaia will watch over us and if I'm not safe with my husband then who would I be safe with?' replied Kira, giving her friend an extra hug.

'I know, you are right. Last minute nerves I guess.' Martha raised her voice. 'Does everyone have their new comms system?' There were nods all round. 'Remember, this is our private channel, make sure you keep it to yourself. You will still be able to contact the other members of Resistance just not on this frequency.'

'We know, Ma. We've been through this a hundred times,' said Dina as she gathered up her things.

'This is it then. Good luck, everyone,' said Jed which triggered a mass hand shaking and hugging event with people getting in each other's way as they tried to make sure they'd said goodbye to everyone.

Max was feeling very forlorn being one of those staying behind. He coughed loudly to get everyone's attention.

'Ahem, everyone, if I could just have a moment.' He cleared his throat again. 'It's been a real pleasure to have gone through this journey with you all. I know that staying here is an important job and I'll make sure the entire base is ready to come out and meet you as soon as you say the word, Jed. I wish we didn't have to be separated, but I know you will all take care of each other and with that in mind...' He bent down to one knee and brought out a box from his jacket pocket. He opened it to reveal a delicate diamond ring. 'Dina Grey, will you marry me?'

Dina looked at him in absolute shock. No-one said anything.

'Dina?' Max faltered.

Then Dina flung herself at him and hugged him tighter than she'd ever hugged anything before. 'YES!' she yelled loudly before smothering his face in kisses. 'Frag, yes!'

Everyone burst into applause and began hugging

each other again while Max, with shaky fingers, put the ring onto Dina's hand.

'Where did you get this?' she asked, admiring the beautiful ring.

'It was my mums and her mums and hers before that. It's been passed down through the family.' Max ran a hand through his hair. 'I've had it in my pocket, waiting for the right time.'

'It's perfect.' Dina hugged him again before the others crowded in, wanting to congratulate the happy couple.

Max caught Artem's elbow. 'Look after her, won't you?'

Artem clapped a hand on Max's back and then spied Zac at the doorway.

'Is time, we go!'

There was a flurry of movement as people got their bags and made their final farewells. Jed shook Zac's hand and wished him good luck before Zac headed out the door with Martha and Lucas, Dina and Artem. Then Jed and Kira, together with their children, went in search of Archer, Simmonds and Kolwowsky down in the skimmer bay, ready to start their own mission. Max and Ash stood silently in the now empty room and regarded each other.

'I suppose we ought to crack on,' said Max.

'Yep, lots to do. I'm headed down to Science and Technology,' replied Ash.

'I have to start my rounds. Talking to the people.'

'Oh, yeah. Right. Good luck with that.'

'Thanks.'

The two men stood for a moment before Ash lifted a hand in farewell and walked out of the quarters to go find his sister.

'Then there was one,' murmured Max, suddenly missing everyone intensely, especially Dina. He keyed the door shut on his way out and brought up the first sector on his handheld, ready to tell them what had to happen next. He hoped his authority was recognised.

Martha hurried down the corridor after Artem, trying to ignore the butterflies in her stomach at the thought of flying. Witnessing the explosion of his compound after they had taken off last time was making her nervous of setting off this time, but she knew rationally that New Corp were not in a position to strike at the Resistance camp. Nothing was going to happen.

They all boarded the plane without incident and found seats. Zac joined Artem again as co-pilot while Martha secured Lucas safely. Dina joined them in the same row leaving Hernandez to do his own thing.

The plane took off without incident.

'Where are we going to land?' Dina whispered to Martha.

'I think Artem is hoping his airstrip is still there. If not, he says he can land the plane on any bare strip of land and let's face it, there are plenty of those.'

'I guess. What if New Corp try to shoot us down?'

'I think if they could do that, they would have done that last time.'

Dina shivered. 'Do you think anyone will listen to us?'

'They have to. We have the facts on our side. If they do not evacuate the island, it will be submerged in water and I am sure they already know about the problem. I find it hard to believe they would let themselves die out of stubbornness.'

'It's not New Corp I'm worried about. It's the people they've left behind,' remarked Dina.

'What do you mean?'

'You seriously think the people in charge don't already have an exit strategy? It wouldn't surprise me to find out that they'd already left.'

Kira, Jed and the children found the others waiting for them in the skimmer bay.

'Finally decided to turn up, did we?' Archer glared at them.

'We're not late, thank you very much,' retorted Kira.

Jed swiftly came in between the two of them. 'Let's get our bags on board, shall we? Then we can set off.'

Kira glared at him but helped Jed to load the bags into the hold. 'Why are you being nice to her?' she hissed at him.

'Because we have to travel with them for at least a week and provide a united front when we get to City 50, which I don't think we'll manage very well if you two are fighting all the time.'

'We're not fighting.'

Jed stared at her.

'Okay, fine. She's snippy and gets under my skin but I will try and ignore her.'

'Thank you, there's a lot riding on this, hon. It's important.' Jed gave her a quick kiss on the cheek.

'I know, I know,' grumbled Kira as she moved round the side of the skimmer to let herself into the vehicle. She secured the children first then made sure she was sat at the back, as far away from Archer as possible.

Kolwowsky was driving and Simmonds kept him company, leaving Jed the difficult choice of sitting with his wife or sitting with Archer. As he climbed into the skimmer, he noticed the chair would swivel. He unlocked it so that he could turn and talk to both women. They both sniffed at him in disapproval then glared at each other.

Giving up, Jed pulled out his handheld and went over all the details Zac had provided about City 50. Anything to avoid being in the middle of Archer and Kira.

The skimmer started off without a hitch and soon they were leaving the base behind.

Chapter Thirty-Three

Kolwowsky had no problems at first following the existing roads as there was limited debris and the surfaces were still driveable. There wasn't much to see out of the window. Kira recognised the same dead landscape as a result of the HER wars and was sad to see that nature had less of a foothold here than she'd noticed back on her island. No wonder Gaia was uncertain of their success.

The only point of interest on the journey were the abandoned husks of large buildings which Kira could only assume had been some kind of place of commerce or maybe a residential block. Her knowledge outside the island was limited. As junior archivist she had access to all the information about cities 9, 15, 42 and 36 on their island and obviously she knew there had been 50 in total, but she had not yet been given clearance at work to learn about them. That would have been the next natural step for her if she'd stayed in City 42. But then, if they'd stayed, they would have been arrested and the children removed from their care. Kira's stomach clenched as she thought about that threat. *Would City 50 uphold such an order?* She tried to take her mind off things by following Jed's example and reading the briefing notes Zac had provided but she'd already tried to read them twice and the words kept dancing around in front of her eyes. She gave up and stared aimlessly out of the window.

Jed glanced at Kira, she seemed to be in a world of her own. Peter and Grace were fast asleep. He turned to see Archer watching him.

'Everything alright?' he asked.

'Peachy.'

'You know, you could try being a bit more approachable. We have an important job to do here. A united front will make us all seem more credible.'

'Zac told me that you all have prices on your head. I hardly think having a united front will do anything about that,' replied Archer.

'But we don't know City 50 is staunchly New Corp, do we?'

'Let's hope not.' Archer angled her body away from Jed as much as possible, sending the very clear signal that she did not want to talk to him anymore. He took the hint and went back to his handheld.

The mood in the skimmer was matched by the weather as dark clouds gathered and rain began falling.

'I think we will have to stop soon; this weather isn't safe for driving. The road is beginning to deteriorate a little and I don't want to have an accident on day one!' joked Kolwowsky. 'Of course, I don't want to have an accident at all, but you know what I mean, right?'

'I think we should push on. We're on a timetable after all. I can help you drive if you like, I don't mind. Simmonds, do you want to swap out?' asked Jed.

Simmonds threw him a dark look but agreed so there was a bit of clambering over limbs and equipment as Jed swapped places with her. Kira was still in a world of her own, half dozing but Archer was pleased her wife was sitting with her.

'Why are you being so hostile?' whispered Simmonds.

'I'm nervous that 50 will turn us away because they're with us.' Archer cast a doubtful look at Kira. 'What do we do if they rescind on our deal? We have nowhere else to go. We can't build another Resistance out there.' She gestured to the wilderness outside the skimmer window. 'We don't have the resources or logistics.'

'They won't turn us away; they are desperate for our technology. Be positive, everything will be alright.' Simmonds smiled at her, but Archer found it difficult to take comfort from the unknown.

Jed convinced Kolwowsky to let him drive for several hours before conditions deteriorated further and they had to stop. The skimmer was anchored to the ground, but the weather was too bad to go outside and set up the proper sleeping pods. Instead they made up makeshift beds within and let the two children crawl around in the middle. Dinner was a simple affair, some bread and cheese. No-one felt like setting up the synth-caf machine, so they drank water.

'Ugh, I want to be there already,' said Kira. 'How much further do we have to go, Kolwowsky?'

'We are about halfway on the roads that we know are passable. After that we have to go on foot. That's when it'll get more difficult. Especially in this weather.' He glanced at the children. 'Do you have rain covers for them?'

'Yeah, the strollers come with inbuilt weather shields. They will keep warm and dry, even if the rest of us aren't.'

'Lucky them,' commented Archer drily. She was

trying not to be interested in what they were doing but Peter was doing his best to undo her boots and his little face as he concentrated was adorable.

'Okay, I'm going to call it a night. Get these two settled. Perhaps we can make it to the end of the road tomorrow and then, best foot forward and all that,' said Kira.

The next day the sun shone down gloriously. It was so nice that Archer approved having the skimmer windows down and the team enjoyed the fresh air as they travelled along. They made great time and found the end of the road easily enough. There was a huge gash in the tarmac and what followed was a mixture of large stones and rubble.

'Looks like there was some kind of landslide or something,' said Jed, looking up at the mountainous landscape. 'That will be why the satellites were reporting no access anymore.'

'Can we get past that?' Kira eyed the boulders nervously.

'Probably not, but we should be able to go around. Hopefully it won't add too much onto our journey.'

'How are you going to push that over those?' Archer asked as she pointed at the stroller and the landslide.

'It has an all-terrain setting, it won't be a problem,' retorted Kira. And she pressed a few buttons on the stroller to get it ready for movement. Large chunky tyres appeared together with shock absorbers.

'These things really are incredible,' murmured Jed.

'You can thank Ingrid, she gave us one,' Kira replied softly and squeezed her husband's hand.

Travelling across the rubble was exciting at first, a

real adventure, but when the terrain didn't get any easier and it didn't look like they were making any headway, tempers grew short.

'Frag it!' exclaimed Kira as the stroller stuck, again. 'This is ridiculous!' She shoved and pushed and tried to lever the baby carrier out of whatever rut it had got jammed into, but nothing moved. She shoved harder and was rewarded with her own feet losing their balance on the rocky surface, and she almost fell. 'Would somebody fragging help me out here?' Kira yelled in frustration.

Archer tutted loudly as she turned back to help and mis-stepped, falling awkwardly to the ground. When she tried to stand her left ankle gave way immediately making her gasp with the pain.

'You are fragging kidding me!' she shouted which got everyone's attention and the others stopped clambering and turned back to help the two women.

Simmonds took out the med kit and applied a numbing shot to her wife's ankle before beginning to expertly strap it up.

'I would say rest and elevation, but I don't think you'll get much of that here.' She tried to lighten the mood but her half-joke fell on deaf ears.

'Just strap the fragging thing up so I can walk,' snapped Archer. She immediately felt guilty and pressed her forehead on Simmonds' shoulder briefly in apology. Five minutes later and she was stood up, gingerly testing her weight on her now numb ankle, held stiffly in place by a sturdy brace.

'The pain killers will last for a couple of hours, but you'll certainly feel it when they wear off. We need to set up camp soon so you can rest. There's still another days hike ahead of us.' Kolwowsky looked worried as he glanced back at Archer and forwards at the trail ahead.

Jed heaved the stroller out of the crevice it had gotten wedged into and Kira was about to apologise to Archer before she saw the women's thunderous gaze. She decided it could wait.

'What about that outcrop?' pointed Jed. The spot looked perfect for camping, but it also looked further than anyone really felt like walking.

'Looks great,' muttered Archer and she headed in that direction.

'I guess that's our campsite then.' Kolwowsky flashed a small grin at the others and followed his commander. Simmonds fell into conversation with him, leaving Kira and Jed to bring up the rear.

'I feel really bad,' Kira said to her husband in a low voice.

'It wasn't your fault. It could've happened to any of us, at any time. Still could,' replied Jed trying to make her feel better. 'Let's get to camp and then you can run around making her dinner and bringing her drinks if it makes you feel any better.'

Kira pressed her lips together in a small smile. She didn't think any of that would be appreciated it, but it might be worth a try. They plodded on up the mountainside, more cautious now than before until finally they reached the flat outcrop Jed had pointed out.

Archer's mood was even blacker than before and no-one really said anything as the camp was set up and various food pouches were rehydrated.

Kira thanked Gaia that the children were subdued and somehow tired from the journey, even though they hadn't done any walking. They went to sleep easily at their normal bedtime and Kira sadly thanked her mum for the advice she had given about setting a routine as early as possible. Wishing she was tramping up the mountain with her, Kira had a few tears in her eyes, and she went to see if there was anything she could do for Archer.

'I'm fine,' Archer said crossly as Kira approached but when she saw the tearful expression on the other woman's face, she relented. 'It wasn't your fault, could've happened to anyone.'

Kira nodded. 'Can I get you anything?'

'I'm good. Thank you.' Archer nodded brusquely and Kira half smiled before returning to her side of the campsite.

The mood remained subdued and it wasn't long before everyone had retired for the night. No-one bothered to sit around the campsite and watch the stars twinkling in the clear night sky.

'Wake-up. Wake-up, Jed. Help me with the kids, please?' Kira shook her husband a little harder than before, willing him to wake up. Peter's nappy had leaked, and the children's bedding was sodden. She hoped that when they arrived at City 50 there would be facilities to wash and dry things.

'I'm awake. I'm awake,' Jed groaned trying to open his eyes and was rewarding with an extremely wiggly Grace as Kira tried to sort out Peter with some dry clothes. By the time she had finished Jed was wide-awake and everyone wanted out of the sleeping pod.

The morning outside was crisp and clear, they could see for miles. Making sure the children were wrapped up warmly in their coats, Kira smiled as Kolwowsky brought her a cup of synth-caf.

'Thank you.'

'No problem. I have some porridge warming. They'll

eat that, won't they?' he nodded towards the children.

'Yeah, should do.'

'Then we'll need to get going if we want to arrive at City 50 before dark.'

'Is it that far then?' Kira was concerned, she hadn't thought they had to walk too much further.

'It's about half a day, but with Archer's ankle and the stroller, it'll probably take longer,' replied Kolwowsky.

'Sorry,' said Kira in a small voice.

'Stop apologising and get packed up. The sooner we can move, the sooner we can get there,' said Archer, not unkindly, as she hobbled past. The drugs had worn off somewhat, but she was waiting until they were ready to move before she took anymore. She was determined to make it to the gates.

Six hours later, she did, and her mood plummeted even further when the gates to City 50 refused to open. Archer hammered on the doors loudly.

'What's going on?' asked Kira, the last to arrive at the gates, pushing and shoving the stroller in front of her. She'd been glad of it as a means of getting the children up the mountain, but she would be grateful if she never had to see it again.

'They won't open the gates,' explained Kolwowsky who was looking very nervous.

Kira spotted a small vid-screen, half hidden by some scrub. 'Have you tried this?' she asked, pushing the vegetation aside.

The screen flickered and a tinny voice issued.

'State your name and purpose for visit to City 50.'

'I am Colonel Archer of the Resistance and I demand that you open the gates!'

Kira winced at Jed; she didn't think that was likely to work.

'Request denied,' came the reply.

'WHAT?' shouted Archer. She was about to jab the screen again when Jed caught her arm.

'Let me try.'

'Why the frag would I do that? You're a civilian.'

'Yes, maybe they'll listen to me.'

Archer scowled and moved slightly out of the way so Jed could access the screen.

'Hello? This is Jed Jenkins requesting entry into City 50. I…' He was cut off by the tinny voice replying.

'Did you say Jenkins?'

'Yes.' Jed waited.

'Are you Gretchen's boy?'

Jed stared at Kira in disbelief before answering yes again.

'You'd better come in.' And with that the gates creaked open.

Archer stared at Jed in consternation. 'Who the bloody hell is Gretchen?'

'One hell of a woman,' replied Jed with a grin and started walking into City 50, closely followed by Kira and the stroller. Kolwowsky scrambled to catch up and Simmonds tugged her wife's arm to get her moving so they could all enter the city together.

Chapter Thirty-Four

Kira and Jed pushed the children's stroller through the gateway and into the corridor, the others not far behind them. They could hear footsteps hurrying towards them and Kira braced herself for whatever was coming. A short woman with olive skin and dark hair that was escaping her attempts at a bun scurried around the corner.

'Ah, you're there. Hello, welcome. Sorry. Security is tight. The 'flu has been devastating. But you're here now so come, come. Follow me.' She didn't wait to see if they were doing as she had requested, she just pivoted and hurried back the way she had come.

Archer scowled at the women's rapidly disappearing back and did her best to hobble after her as quickly as possible.

'Excuse me!' she called. 'Are you Bridget? Bridget Mulhurne? We are expected. We have an agreement.'

The woman stopped abruptly and without turning around spoke softly.

'Bridget is dead. Please, you must come with me.'

Kira's stomach sank. The woman Zac had made the agreement with was dead.

'What does that mean?' she whispered to Jed, but

Archer overheard her.

'It means we need to work out a new agreement, fast.' Without waiting for them, Archer scrambled after the mystery woman, determined to find out what was going on.

They rounded a corner and were faced with a decontamination chamber.

'You understand,' the woman half-smiled apologetically. 'We can't let you in unless you've been decontaminated. On the other side you'll find clean clothes and 'flu shots. You must administer them otherwise you cannot enter the city. Alright?' She waited to see whether there would be any disagreement.

'Do you know about our agreement with City 50?' asked Archer brusquely.

'A lot of things have changed since then. The city is in flux. But we can talk about it afterwards. Please.' The woman begged with her entire demeanour.

'What's your name?' asked Kira kindly. 'I'm Kira Jenkins, and this is my husband Jed and our children Grace and Peter.'

'Monique. My name's Monique but please, you must decontaminate before I can talk to you any further.' And she cast one last desperate glance at them before stepping through a side door which locked with an audible click behind her.

'I guess we decontaminate then,' said Jed. 'What do we do?'

A voice crackled through speakers that were located above the door Monique had walked through.

'Walk through the double doors and listen to the instructions. One at a time, please.'

'I'm going first,' snarled Archer and she pushed through the doors without waiting to hear what anyone else thought.

'Kolwowsky, you go second and sort out the 'flu shots on the other side. Simmonds you follow and I'll bring up the rear. You go before me with the children, Kira – is that alright? Can you manage?'

'Yes, we'll be fine.'

No-one said anything else while they each waited their turn to go through the decontamination chamber. Kira wondered where they had unearthed this kind of technology from but remembered that City 50 was meant to be the pinnacle of all of New Corp's research science and technology plus everything the planet's history had to offer. She guessed they had access to all the archive material plus the intelligent minds needed to put it all together.

As she walked through the double doors, pushing the stroller in front of her, Kira was struck by how clinical it smelt within. There was a huge gush of air and smoke, which made her cough a little and startled the children enough to make them cry. Kira bent down to them both and gave them a hug, murmuring words of comfort. She became aware of a blue glow and glanced up to see if it was part of the process.

Gaia stood before her, smaller and more transparent than she'd ever looked before but with the same sad smile. She lifted her hand, and it seemed to coalesce into something more solid and once it was fully materialised, the goddess gently reached out and touched each child with a finger, sending a golden glow briefly through them.

'Are we safe?' whispered Kira.

Gaia smiled at her and then looked down at the children. Kira followed her gaze and somehow knew Grace and Peter would be fine against the 'flu or any other illness that might be lurking within City 50.

'Thank you,' she said, raising her head to look at Gaia but the goddess was gone and the doors on the other side were opening.

Kolwowsky beckoned her to come through, armed with the 'flu shot.

'The children don't need it,' Kira said in a daze, not entirely sure what to make of what happened.

Kolwowsky took no notice and administered it to them anyway. 'Better to be on the safe side,' he said chirpily.

Jed joined them, and once he'd been inoculated, Monique reappeared. This time with a more welcoming look on her face.

'Thank you. We can't be too careful. You know how it is. If you will follow me?'

'Where to this time?' asked Archer. 'I want some answers.'

'I'm going to take you to the city council, there's not many of us left after the epidemic but there's someone who wants to talk to you. Well, one of you anyway.' Monique darted a glance at Jed but said nothing else.

'And does this so-called council have the power to reinstate our agreement with City 50?' demanded Archer.

'It does. If you have anything worth bringing us.' Monique gestured to the open door, effectively cutting off the opportunity for more conversation.

A steadying arm from Simmonds prevented Archer from saying anymore, but she wasn't happy and muttered under her breath about jumped up council members with no authority all the way to the room Monique was taking them.

Monique ushered them into the small meeting room where three people sat waiting for them. A smiling man, a very timid looking woman who nervously adjusted her spectacles and a young girl who looked barely out of her teenage years.

'Here they are,' she said. 'This is Jed Jenkins.' And she pointed at him.

The man leapt up and grabbed Jed's hand, shaking it enthusiastically. He was entirely bald but maintained a neat goatee and put Jed immediately at ease with his cheerful manner.

'So pleased to meet you.' He turned to Kira. 'And you must be Kira, and here are the children. Such poppets. I'm Richard. I'm one of the people sort of in charge after everything that happened.'

'I'm Colonel Archer, this is Captain Simmonds and Lieutenant Kolwowsky from the Resistance. We had an agreement in place with Bridget Mulherne. I understand you can ratify that agreement?' Archer wasted no time in getting down to business.

'We can. If, of course, you can bring us anything of value,' replied the teenage girl.

Archer stiffened and was about to reply until Jed cut across her.

'We do, but first let's finish the introductions and find out how you know who I, who we, are?' He pointed at his wife and flashed a smile at the two women sat across the table.

'I'm Liss. I'm the oldest of the children left. I speak for them,' replied the teenage girl.

'And I'm Olive. I represent the women and the elder residents. The ones who survived the 'flu, that is,' said the older woman in a quiet voice.

'As I said, I'm Richard. I represent the men and the workforce. I speak with the authority of New Corp although...' he scratched behind his ear and glanced at the others before continuing. 'Although New Corp seem to have disappeared.'

'Disappeared? What do you mean?' interrupted Archer.

'They were supposed to come here. The people in charge. They left City 42 but there was a big storm at sea and the plane went down. All lives lost. We're what's left.' Richard coughed nervously.

'Who was supposed to come here? And you still haven't told us how you know who we are?' asked Jed before Archer could say anything else. She glared daggers at him.

'Bridget, you know Bridget, she was friends with your mother, Gretchen. She sent a message over there to let Gretchen know about the 'flu and to request help only she never survived to get the reply.'

'She knew my mother?' Jed was surprised. He'd never considered the possibility that his mother really knew anyone important at all.

'Yes. It was Gretchen who told us about the high-ranking officials leaving the island and coming here. We were able to monitor their flight until the storm hit. Sad, really.'

'Not especially,' commented Archer. 'Do you mean to say that an incredibly convenient storm wiped out the board of directors from New Corp and there's nobody left to challenge that authority?'

'Well… yes.' Richard walked over to the wall and tapped the vid-screen. A map of the region appeared. The landmass shown started to shrink as the water levels rose rapidly. 'You are aware of the current situation, aren't you? That's why you're here, isn't it?. To get away from the rising sea level. Although, I rather thought there would be a few more of you.'

'We're the advance party,' commented Archer sourly. 'And yes, we are aware of the imminent environmental disaster. It's why we've left our base and travelled here. Why General Ridgely made the agreement with Mulherne to settle our people here.'

'So you are bringing the AIs then?' asked Liss eagerly.

'And the seed bank?' queried Olive.

'We are. Provided there is a place for our people here.' Archer tilted her chin in challenge at the delegates from City 50.

'How many of you are there?' asked Richard.

'About five hundred plus the people from City 42 and City 9. If they come.'

'What do you mean if they come?' Olive asked, pushing her glasses up her nose.

This time Jed answered. 'We've sent a delegation over to the island to see whether the people want to come back with us. To come to safety. We didn't want to leave anyone behind.' He paused briefly. 'So, my mother. Are you still in touch with her? Is she alright? Can I speak with her?'

'Ah, we've lost connection with the Governor's office, but have no fear, your mother is one of the most capable women I've ever met. I have no doubt that she has a plan a foot.' Richard smiled but it didn't quite mask the worry in his eyes.

'Sorry, Governor?' asked Kira.

'Oh yes, Gretchen was made Governor after New Corp took back control. She kept a steady hand on things over there.'

Archer interrupted again. 'So are you New Corp or aren't you?'

'Not really,' said Olive, glancing at the others. 'We're

sort of what's left.'

'And why are you so divided? Representing the men, the women, the children?' asked Kira. She felt uneasy at those divisions.

'It just sort of happened. When we realised that people were dropping like flies, we set up chains of command for those that were left and it sort of devolved into what you see now,' replied Richard.

'How long have you had the epidemic?' asked Kira.

Richard glanced at the others for confirmation. 'About six months?' They nodded. 'About six months, all in. It came in waves.' He coughed nervously. 'It's been devastating really. Truly devastating.'

'Is it under control now?' Kira was worried.

'Oh yes,' Monique replied. She had stayed quiet in deference to the council leaders. 'I'm in admin. I keep an eye on the numbers and things. We haven't had a 'flu related death in nearly two weeks.'

Kira clutched the stroller handle tighter. That didn't fill her with much confidence. She bent down slightly to check on the children. They were oddly quiet.

'We have an agreement then. Our people can come and settle here, in City 50. We share the AI technology and our seed bank with you while you provide homes, jobs, medicine for us. The deal General Ridgely and Bridget Mulherne made.' Archer was keen to clarify an agreement had been made.

'Any objections?' Richard asked the others from City 50. They both shook their heads. 'We are agreed. Do we shake on it?' He was feeling relieved that new technology and a new food source would be coming, plus an influx of new, healthy people.

Archer held out a hand stiffly and Richard shook it vigorously.

'Should I draw up an agreement for everyone to sign?' asked Monique.

'I think that would be an excellent idea,' replied Jed.

'Can we get access to a communications array?' asked Archer. She was keen to get on with the mission. 'I want to update our teams and get things moving from the base, get our people up here.'

'I'll show you,' said Liss and she bounced up from the chair. Simmonds fell in behind Archer, motioning Kolwowsky to stay put.

Both soldiers been quiet during the exchange, adhering to the chain of command, but as soon as Archer left the room, Kolwowsky had his own questions for Monique about how she was running the city and the procedures she had in place. Kira smiled fondly as she watched the two of them, heads together, discussing the different ways they handled large groups of people.

'Could we have somewhere to freshen up? To feed the children?' Jed asked Richard.

'Yes, of course! Follow me, we'll get you some food and drink, get you settled in. Show you round. Whatever you want,' replied Richard eagerly.

Kira smiled at Olive who returned it tentatively and half waved as the family left the room. Kira was both curious and apprehensive at what they would see.

Chapter Thirty-Five

'How is the AI move coming along?' asked Max as he, Ash, Bennett, Dr Glover and Lieutenant Yarrow met for their daily meeting. It had been Max's idea that they check in regularly with their progress so any problems could be dealt with as soon as they occurred.

'I can't prevent the memory loss. We've been able to create transportable drives for all the AIs and their function will be unaffected, but they won't remember previous actions they have carried out. The longer they're being transported the greater the memory loss,' replied Glover.

'Is that really an issue though?' Bennett wasn't bothered about the loss of memory. As far as she was concerned the AIs could stay at the base.

'What if it affects their ability to carry out the tasks they were designed for? Is that likely?' asked Max.

'No, their base programming won't be affected. They might not remember having carried out the task before though.'

Bennett interrupted. 'So why are we worried about the memory loss then? Seems pointless.'

Glover huffed at her. 'Because, the AIs are designed to learn as they carry out their tasks. They adapt to their workload and user interfaces coming up with unique solutions.'

'Or new ways to destroy my plants,' muttered Bennett, but the only one who heard her was Max and he smothered a smile.

'The real question is when we download them. I really think we should wait until the last minute and there is the question of order – which AI should be left online until the last possible moment?' Ash looked around at the others. 'What do you think?'

'Surely Frank should be last. He's in charge of all the stores and keeping track of our supplies, we'll need him right up until the last moment,' suggested Max.

'No, Layla should be last. She's the one plugged into the most systems. She will be the one to warn us if anything goes wrong or if there's an external attack. She monitors the perimeter as well as holding all the plans for our tech if something should go wrong. We leave her to last.' Glover was adamant.

'Can you not download both of them last?' Ash couldn't really see the problem.

'Does it even matter?' asked Bennett. 'The important thing is my plants; we need more manpower to help with the transport. Have we heard back from the team that went to City 50? Are they going to let us in?'

'Yes, it does matter, Bennett. My AIs are extremely intricate pieces of technology that are guaranteeing us a place in City 50. Without them we wouldn't get in the gates,' retorted Glover.

'Can't eat 'em though, can you? It's my seed bank that'll get us in.'

'Ahem!' It was Ash. 'We have had a communique from Archer. They've arrived safely and things aren't exactly what they expected. It seems the city was hit hard with the 'flu and they've lost about fifty per cent of the population. They're grateful to have us. The seeds and the tech are more a bonus than a deal breaker, from what Archer said.'

'Any word from the team that went back?' Max tried and failed to hide his worry.

'Nothing yet, but I'm sure they're okay. Artem will look after them.'

'What about New Corp? Are they in control in 50 or what?' Bennett scowled at Ash.

'Apparently not.'

There was a brief silence as everyone digested that piece of news.

'Just going back to your manpower issue, Bennett, the people in G-block are refusing to leave so…'

Bennett interrupted. 'I'm not leaving any plants behind.'

'No, and I'm not leaving an AI or any tech. We're taking everything with us. They're fools to stay behind.' For once Glover and Bennett agreed on something.

'Be that as it may, I thought if we asked them to help on a project, it might encourage them to change their minds. I'm going to assign them over to Allotment but don't give them a hard time about not wanting to leave, Bennett. This is scary stuff.'

Bennett nodded briefly then stood. 'If there's nothing else?'

The others shook their heads and watched as the feisty gardener left the room.

'I still think Layla should be last for download,' Glover said quietly.

'Oh, for frag's sake, sis! We can do Frank AND Layla last. Stop being difficult.' Ash was semi-serious.

Glover blinked at him in surprise and then half

smiled.

'Now that we know we are welcome in City 50, I can't see any reason to delay things,' said Max. 'I think we should start the move.'

The mood of the room shifted.

'Are we really doing this?' asked Ash.

Max nodded and sighed. 'If I take G-block over to Allotment, I'll give Bennett the nod to start moving. She's ready and it'll be better for her to go first. She can take all the people not assigned to a specific job with her -that'll give her all the manpower she'll need.'

'And it will encourage the others to get their arses in gear, I like it!' Glover was grinning. 'Speaking of which, I'd better make sure all the technicians are packed up. They do a bit, then get distracted by a new idea and end up unpacking everything to find a particular part.'

'You're awfully quiet, Yarrow. Anything to report?' asked Max.

'Peacekeepers are ready to move, Sir.' He didn't salute, but it was implied by his tone.

'Okay, good. Let's split the peacekeepers up and get a group of techies, plants and residents moving together with a couple of peacekeepers. Actually, that's probably something Layla could put together for us.' Max turned to Glover.

You are correct, Dr Carter. List created.

There was a ping on everyone's handhelds and indeed, the lists had been created. Max had a quick scroll through.

'Looks good to me, everyone happy?'

There were nods and a *Yes, Sir* from Yarrow.

'Let's get it done then.' Max scratched his head. 'Feels a bit odd, doesn't it? An anti-climax almost.'

'I don't think it's really sunk in for a lot of people.

It'll be real now and we might find there's more resistance to the move. Maybe I could come and do the rounds with you, Max? Help ease some worries,' suggested Ash.

'That would be great. I'm doing A, B and C block this morning, if you're up for it?'

Ash nodded and the two men stood, closely followed by Yarrow and Glover.

'Unless there are any disasters, let's check in tomorrow first thing,' said Max and after waiting for confirmation from the others, he and Ash left the room, headed to A-Block.

Chapter Thirty-Six

'Do you think we can trust Artem?' Dina asked Martha quietly. They were sitting together on Artem's plane, travelling back to the island.

Martha glanced at Hernandez before replying. He wasn't paying them any attention.

'I think so. I mean, why would we not?'

Dina sighed.

'His complex was blown up as we left – how do we know it was New Corp? That's just what Artem said.'

Martha's eyes were wide in disbelief.

'You cannot be seriously considering that Artem blew up his complex himself. Ruth and Sarah were there. He would not,' she whispered. 'He could not. He was overjoyed to see her again. And killing a child knowingly… no, I do not believe he is capable of that.'

Dina twisted her hands around in her lap.

'Yeah, okay so maybe not that but… I dunno, something is a bit… off. Don't you think?'

Martha was shaking her head.

'You cannot look for conspiracies everywhere you go, Dina. He has been a good friend to us. He helped look after Kira when she was struggling with her grief, and Jed does not have a bad word to say about him.

Unless you have solid proof of something, I think you need to let this go.' Martha said sternly.

Flushing Dina nodded, unwilling to say anymore. She still had her niggle, but she was hoping it was just paranoia sending her into suspicious overdrive.

'Attention. Seatbelts, please. We're coming into land.' Artem's voice crackled over the intercom and all the passengers complied. They could see the remains of the compound out of the window. It was mostly rubble with the odd half wall here and there. Nature was already taking over in a couple of places as the plants from the garden were spreading.

The plane came into land easily. Artem's runway had been untouched by the destruction. He ducked out of the cockpit, followed by Zac.

'I go, very quick. Back very soon.' And he didn't wait for a response. They all watched him exit the plane.

'Should one of us go with him?' asked Martha.

Zac shook his head.

'He wants to get some tech that was in the safe room. He won't be long.'

'I don't care what he's going in for. I'm going too.' And before anyone could stop her, Dina had leapt out of her seat and quickly darted out of the plane.

'Frag!' exclaimed Martha, as she fumbled with her belt and in her haste, scared Lucas who began to cry.

'Relax, I'll go after her,' offered Zac.

'No! Wait for us. We are coming.' Martha had managed to get out of her seat and picked up Lucas and was manhandling the travel cube up the aisle, ready to expand it outside. 'Come on, let's get after her.'

There was no sign of Artem, but Martha could see Dina's blonde head bobbing about.

'What is she doing?' muttered Martha.

'She's checking the bodies,' replied Zac and offered her a small smile of comfort.

Martha increased her pace to try and catch up with her friend when she saw her head bob down and not come back up again.

'Dina? Dina?' Martha called.

'Here. I'm here.'

Skirting a pile of rubble, Martha stopped short as she took in the scene. Dina was kneeling on the floor in front of some charred remains. There was nothing to identify who the person had been apart from a smaller, blackened skeleton within its arms.

'Oh,' exclaimed Martha softly and felt her legs go weak. She dropped down to join Dina, oblivious to Lucas and Zac nearby. She didn't make a sound as tears rolled down her face.

Dina found her hand and clung to it.

'I want to bury them,' she said quietly.

'I'll go find some shovels,' Zac offered and hurried off in the direction of the gardener's shed, or at least where he thought the gardener's shed had been. A quick search and miraculously it was still standing. He pulled the door open and was relieved to find a couple of shovels. He grabbed them quickly and hurried back to the women.

When he got there, Artem had arrived and was stood, stock still, all colour drained from his face. He looked up at Zac's arrival.

'I thought… I thought… there was safe room and… I hoped…' He couldn't say anymore but noticed the shovels in Zac's hand. 'I dig.' And he held out a hand.

Dina leapt up and grabbed the other shovel from Zac's hand, glaring at him so fiercely he didn't voice any objections.

Artem had started digging and Dina got stuck in. The two of them made it look like a competition as to who could dig faster. It didn't take long for a grave to be dug. Both of them stood panting heavily, leaning on their shovels.

Martha motioned Zac to stay back and she gingerly picked up the skeletons. They were brittle but thankfully didn't break apart and she was able to lower them into the earth.

'Flowers,' Dina said abruptly. 'They need flowers.'

Everyone began looking and easily found patches of wildflowers nearby. Soon the two skeletons were wreathed in blooms that by rights shouldn't have been there that time of year.

'Gaia's touch,' murmured Martha and Dina nodded in agreement.

Artem and Dina shovelled the earth back into the ground, slower this time and with audible sobs and visible shoulder shakes from both of them.

'Do you want to say anything?' Martha asked the two of them.

'She was my friend; my family; she didn't deserve this.' Dina wanted to say more but her voice broke and she shook her head, unable to continue.

'My Ruthie,' rumbled Artem, tears coursing down his cheeks. 'Is too much.' Abruptly he walked away, shoulders bowed in grief.

'May Gaia hold you in her heart and grant you peace,' whispered Martha. She bent to touch the soil with one hand. A tear splashed down and a small shoot sprang out of the ground. It grew into a small, thorny bush and bloomed into white roses. A bee came out of nowhere and alighted on one of the flowers briefly before buzzing away.

'Wow,' breathed Zac. 'That was…'

'Gaia,' finished Martha.

Dina touched a petal with one finger and then turned away from the grave. She looked pale and had a dirty mark on one cheek.

'Are you okay?' Martha asked.

'No. But we need to go before anyone realises we're here.' Dina squared her shoulders and took a deep, shuddering breath. 'I miss her.'

'We all do,' Martha replied, her voice cracking, and she pulled the younger woman into a hug. They clung to each other for a few moments before Lucas started calling for his mum-mum. 'Come on,' Martha sniffed loudly and wiped her face with her hands. 'Let's go.'

Dina nodded and shoved her hands into her pockets. She wished Max were here.

Back at the plane, a very subdued Artem was waiting for them.

'9 or 42?' he asked.

'I think we should go to 42 first. We know the city and we stand a better chance of convincing the citizens of City 9 to come with us if we have City 42 behind us,' replied Martha.

'Da. We go.' The Russian didn't wait for any further communication and climbed into the plane and through to the cockpit.

The others hurried to get on board as the engines whirred into life.

'Is there even an airstrip near the city?' Dina asked Martha.

'No, but there is plenty of flat land. Artem should not have any problem finding somewhere.'

'What are we going to do when we get there?'

'Hope.' Martha's face was grim. She was determined

to save as many people as she could and find justice for Ruth and Sarah's killers. Someone was going to pay.

Chapter Thirty-Seven

Artem landed the plane on some flat ground outside the City 42. They walked through the city gates in silence, Martha pushing Lucas in his stroller. The gates were open, which she took as a good sign, but her hopes were soon dashed as an armed drone flew around the street corner and aimed its lasers on them. She immediately activated the protection dome on the stroller and stood in front of her child.

You are in violation of sector 17. Lay down your weapons immediately.

Before any of them could comply, they heard the stomp, stomp, stomp of swiftly approaching feet and a squad of New Corp Security came barrelling around the corner, their lasers pointing at the group.

'I demand to see whoever is in charge,' said Martha trying to sound braver than she felt. Instantly multiple laser sights focused on her and her alone.

'You will lay down your weapons and prepare to be searched,' barked the voice of one of the security detail.

Martha nodded and held her arms up. She wasn't carrying a weapon anyway. The others hesitated briefly then complied, even Artem. A swift search took away all their weapons and communications devices then everyone was magno-bound with their hands behind their backs.

'You need to release me so I can push my child's stroller.' Martha's panic rose. Lucas wasn't crying yet, he was too shocked, but it wouldn't be long before all the strange people and noises caused him to wail loudly.

'Take the child,' ordered one of the men.

'NO!' shouted Martha and struggled with her bound hands.

'If you touch one hair on the head of that child, I will fragging kill you!' It was Zac, speaking with such deadly menace that he stopped the guard from moving towards Lucas.

'Please. Let me push him,' begged Martha.

'Fine. Hook her to the stroller and round them up!' barked the man in charge. One of the security officers undid Martha's magno-binders and cuffed her to the stroller. She gave a shaky yet grateful smile to Zac, relieved that no-one had taken her baby away. She left the shield in place.

Lucas cast a worried look at his mummy and began sucking his pacifier in comfort, looking wide-eyed at everyone and everything around him.

The group were hustled into the middle of a ring of security guards and frog-marched through the city. The drone followed them the entire way.

They were taken to Corporation Towers, where the governor offices were still located, ushered into a room with one desk and one chair and left alone, the magno-binders still attached.

Martha released the protective shield from the stroller and managed to lift her son out, with her free arm, for a hug, whispering words of comfort to him.

'This isn't exactly what I was expecting,' said Zac.

'No? It's exactly what I thought would happen,' replied Dina, gloomily. She flinched as the door banged open and Sean came through.

Martha lifted her chin, prepared for whatever venom her former member of staff was about to spew, but he ignored her completely and instead walked over to Artem.

'Misner! Good to see you. Let's get you out of these. Come on, the Governor wants a report.'

The others looked on in shock as Artem's magnobinders were unlocked and he wordlessly followed Sean out of the room.

'What the frag?' exploded Dina. She rounded on Zac and Martha. 'I told you we couldn't trust that fragging Russian!' But she stopped venting when she registered the shocked looks on both their faces.

Lucas began crying. His auntie had scared him.

'Oh, I'm sorry, little man. It's okay,' Dina said as she tried to comfort him.

'All this time,' whispered Zac. He sat heavily in the only chair; disbelief etched all over his face.

Martha started pacing, jigging Lucas as she walked.

'At least we know one thing,' she said.

'What?' asked Dina bitterly.

'Sean's not in charge.'

Dina shrugged. That didn't seem to make much of a difference at the moment.

The door banged open again and this time someone none of them knew scurried in with keys to the magnobinders, and behind them came Gretchen Jenkins, looking as elegant and immaculate as always.

'Martha, good to see you. I must apologise for Sean. He should have released all of you.'

'Gretchen. Are you… are you in charge?' Martha

was the first to speak.

Gretchen patted her hair before replying.

'As much as there's anything to be in charge of. Come. We have a lot to discuss.' She swept out of the room, not waiting to see if the four of them followed her.

'Hernandez, keep your eyes and ears open,' muttered Zac to the soldier. They might not have their weapons, but they were far from defenceless.

'Where are we going?' wondered Dina.

'Looks like we're heading to the main meeting room. This should be interesting.'

Martha was right. Gretchen pushed open a door leading to the meeting room and strode inside. The others hurried to follow her. Martha slowed when she saw Artem and Sean in the room, chatting quietly over synth-caf. She chose to ignore them both and sat down on the opposite side of the room from them, getting Lucas comfortable in her lap.

'Let me start by apologising again for the manner in which you were greeted when you arrived at the city. Things have been in flux lately. Allow me to formally introduce myself to those who don't know me. I am Gretchen Jenkins, current governor to City 42. You probably know me as Jed's mother.' She paused. 'If you would?'

Martha spoke for all of them.

'You know me and my son, Lucas. This is Dina Grey, my friend and former citizen of City 42. This is General Zac Ridgely and Lieutenant Hernandez of the Resistance. Apparently, you already know Artem.' She refused to look in his direction.

'Why are you here?' Gretchen wasted no time in getting down to business.

'You know about the imminent environmental

crisis?' Martha asked.

Gretchen nodded impatiently.

'We're here to offer the hand of peace and the chance to travel to a safe place, City 50.'

Sean made a loud scoffing noise.

'City 50 is plagued with the 'flu. There are no survivors.'

'You should check your facts, Sean. The city has lost half its population and has agreed to take in anyone and everyone who can travel there before the water level rises.' Martha still refused to look at him.

'How do you know that?'

'We have been in communication with a team of people we sent to City 50,' replied Martha, trying to stay calm.

'Is Bridget safe?' Gretchen asked in concern. She'd been unable to raise the woman after receiving her emergency message.

'She did not survive the 'flu. I'm sorry.'

'My son? My grandchildren?'

Relieved to have better news, Martha smiled. 'Yes. Jed, Kira and the children are all safe. They are in City 50 waiting for us, and for you, to join them.'

'How are we going to get there?' Gretchen pointed out of the window. 'We don't exactly have a lot of suitable transport.'

'Artem has a plane. It can carry about fifty people. The rest will have to travel down to City 9. We know they have ships in their harbour, we should be able to mobilise some of them across the water,' Martha explained.

'And then?'

'And then they have to walk. But it is only a few day's journey...'

Sean interrupted before Martha could carry on.

'Only a few days? Is it even safe to be walking about out there? What about radiation levels?' He glanced at Gretchen. 'Surely it's safer for us to stay here. Ride it out.'

'Ride what out? The entire planet's oceans rising to cover most of this island's land mass? How exactly do you plan to ride that out?' Dina was incredulous.

'Is no matter. They want to stay, let them. I want to know one thing.' Artem's tone was quiet yet commanding. Everyone in the room noted the veiled threat behind his words. Everyone apart from Sean.

'And what is that, Misner?' Sean was dismissive.

'Who pushed button on destruction of complex?'

'Those decisions were made by Clarity Jones, head of New Corp. But she's already left. She and her cronies took the only plane available and left the rest of us here.'

'She gave order but who pressed button?'

'Look, I don't like your tone, Misner. You've been paid well for sharing information from your communications array.'

'Who. Pressed. Button?'

Sean took a step back.

'Me, alright. I pressed the button, but I was only following orders. It's Clarity who's really at fault.'

Before anyone else had chance to respond, Artem reached out with both arms and broke Sean's neck. As the man fell dead to the floor there were audible gasps around the room. A New Corp Security guard made to get out his weapon, but Gretchen stopped him.

'Stand down!' She then addressed Artem directly. 'Feel better?'

The Russian nodded.

'I trust the rest of our necks are safe?'

'Da. It was for my Ruthie and Sarah.'

Gretchen continued in a softer tone.

'I did hear about the aftermath. I am terribly sorry for your loss. It was a tragedy that should never have happened.'

Artem merely nodded.

Zac had moved into a protective position in front of Martha, Lucas and Dina while Hernandez was covering the other security guard.

'I have a list of vital community members I'd like to see on that plane,' said Gretchen.

'When you say vital, who does that cover?' Martha was shaken but tried to focus on the task in front of her.

'Medics, technicians and of course the babies from the labs and their carer's. I don't think they should have to trek down to City 9.'

'No, they shouldn't,' agreed Dina. 'But you ought to send a couple of medical staff with those travelling to 9, in case of any disasters.'

'And I think you should come with us, you and your husband,' said Martha. 'I know Jed would like to see you both safe.'

'Quite. I forget, does Kira have any family left in the city?'

'No.' Martha paused. 'They also died in the compound attack.'

Gretchen put a hand to her mouth. She didn't travel in the same social circles as Kira's parents and never had much to do with them outside of family events, but she had liked Jean and Malcolm. Now she would never get to know them any better.

'We should get to work,' said Zac. 'We don't have much time.'

'Yes. Agreed. This is the list for the plane.' Gretchen

tapped a few keys on her handheld and the file was sent over to everyone in the room.

Now that they were back in City 42, they were automatically re-connected to the sweeps and message system.

'I think you should round those people up while I send out a sweep to everyone else to meet in Main Square in an hour. Then I can tell them happens next.' Gretchen cast an eye over the room. 'Shall we meet back at your plane in two hours?'

'How do you know where the plane is?' asked Dina.

'I am not without my resources. But don't worry, the rest of the city have no idea. You won't be bombarded with additional passengers.'

'Provided nobody talks,' muttered Dina but everyone else either didn't hear her or chose to ignore her.

There was a general bustling as people got ready to do what they needed to do until Dina suddenly cried out in alarm.

'What? What is it?' asked Zac.

'Camp Eden! We almost forgot Camp Eden. We have to go get Moham and the others. They have to be on the plane. For Max and the plants.'

'Okay. Take a skimmer, get out there and round them up and meet back at the plane. Do you feel comfortable doing that?' Martha waited for Dina to nod her agreement before she turned to Zac and Hernandez. 'I think we should go together. Nobody knows who you are. I used to be their governor. We stand a slightly better chance of people listening to me.'

There were nods all around.

'What about me?' asked Artem.

'I can use you in the square. People will panic, you can help comfort them.' Gretchen was almost smiling as

she spoke, and he nodded in agreement. 'We meet back
at the plane in two hours. Good luck.'

Chapter Thirty-Eight

Dina arrived back to the plane first. Her skimmer was full with Moham, the other scientists from Camp Eden, and as much equipment and food that they could squeeze in. It had been a wrench to leave the beautiful orchard behind, but they didn't have the time to remove the trees.

There was excited chatter as the Camp Eden team ferried their stuff onto the plane. Dina tried not to worry but she was keeping an eye out for Martha and the others, hoping they would turn up at any moment.

Eventually, Martha, Zac, Hernandez and about thirty people came walking into view. They were all carrying multiple boxes and bags.

'Will we have enough room for all this equipment?' Dina asked Martha as they drew closer.

'It should fit in the hold. Provided we secure it properly, it won't be a problem,' replied Zac. 'Is Artem back?'

'No, he and Gretchen haven't turned up yet.' Dina cast an eye over all the people milling about. 'I think we should get everyone loaded up as quickly as possible. If anyone from the city happens to come this way, it's going to be pretty obvious what's happening, and the plane only has limited space.'

Zac began organising people, getting them to put their non-essential things in the hold where Hernandez was carefully securing everything, and then directing people to board the plane. Martha acted as air-stewardess making sure everyone got a seat while Dina scurried around helping people find lost items and reassuring them about the journey ahead.

Soon everyone was boarded and all they could do was wait. It was now half an hour after the agreed two-hour meeting time. Zac, Martha and Dina were huddled in the doorway of the plane, scanning the horizon for any sign of Artem or Gretchen. Hernandez was already seated inside.

A moving speck appeared in the distance.

'I think that is them,' said Martha.

'I'll get the pre-flight checks done,' said Zac. 'In case we have to make a quick getaway.' And he ducked back inside the plane, heading for the cockpit.

Dina squinted. 'It doesn't look like they were followed by anyone. I can only see one skimmer.'

'That's something, then.'

The skimmer pulled up to the side of the plane and Artem bounded out. He ran up the stairs, flashed a smile at the two women before heading for the cockpit.

Gretchen got out of the skimmer and stood at the base of the steps; her hands folded in front of her.

'How did it go?' called Martha.

'There was general panic, as expected, but the majority of citizens understand that, for their own safety, they need to leave the island.'

'No-one is staying behind?'

'No.'

Martha frowned. 'There is a but, isn't there?'

Gretchen sighed and nodded. She glanced back at

the city in the distance.

'The people wanted guarantees, so I and my husband will be travelling with them.'

'You can't! What about your safety? What about Jed and your family?' Dina was really surprised. She hadn't expected this.

'I am the leader of City 42. I must lead by example. My son will understand that.' Gretchen sniffed. 'And anyway, if I can't trust the journey to be safe – how can I expect anyone else to make it?'

Martha was nodding.

'It makes sense. I just wish there were another way.'

'Believe me, so do I. But I know people in City 9. People with some influence. Perhaps I can help convince them to leave with us.'

'What if they do not want to leave?' asked Martha.

Gretchen shrugged slightly.

'Then we must wish them well and leave them behind. There is enough room for everyone on the boat, but we don't have the luxury of weeks to convince people.'

'Is there a boat available then?'

'Da.' It was Artem. He made Dina jump when he spoke which made him chuckle. 'Is okay. I have boat.'

'Of course you do,' remarked Martha wryly.

'I sail boat. Bring people to 50. Is no problem.'

'But what about the plane? Who's going to fly the plane?' Dina asked in a panic. 'We can't wait for you to come back, can we?'

Artem pushed himself gently past the women standing in the doorway and joined Gretchen at the foot of the steps.

'I'm flying the plane,' said Zac, making Dina jump again as he spoke from behind her.

'Do you know how?' asked Martha in surprise.

'I do. I've flown a little here and there, but this will be my first proper flight on my own.' Zac was pale but resolute.

'Frag's sake,' whispered Dina.

There was an uncomfortable silence before Gretchen clapped her hands.

Dina jumped yet again, making the others smile.

'Sorry,' she grinned in embarrassment. 'I guess I'm feeling nervous.'

'There's no point in dithering. You should all return to your base camp and we should get the city ready to leave.'

'You will keep in touch? Let us know how you're getting on?' asked Martha, coming down the steps, the others following her.

'Of course. I look forward to seeing you all in City 50. We won't be far behind you. There's no time to lose.' Gretchen leaned forward and gave Martha a stiff hug before waving the others goodbye and heading back to the skimmer.

Artem was less restrained. He bearhugged them all.

'Safe travels, my friends. I will see you on the other side.'

Dina watched him hurry over to the skimmer.

'It feels like we might never see them again,' she said in a small voice.

Martha gave her a quick hug around the shoulders.

'Do not think like that. We will all be together again soon. Come on, it is time to go.'

Dina sat with Hernandez, who had saved them a couple of seats, and was tickling Lucas making him giggle.

'Are you sure you can handle this?' Martha asked

Zac.

'Honestly? I don't think I've ever been this scared before in my entire life.'

'Do you want me to sit with you?'

Zac smiled at her. 'That would be amazing. Thank you.' He leant forward and gave her a gentle kiss on the cheek before going through to the cockpit.

Martha blushed a little and darted a glance at Dina, who had been watching. She gave Martha a thumbs up making her blush even more.

Chapter Thirty-Nine

The flight back to the Resistance base was uneventful. Lucas slept and many of the passengers dozed or sat absorbed by their own thoughts. Dina was the first person off the plane, and she dashed into Max's waiting embrace.

'I missed you,' he said as he held her tight. 'Are you alright?'

'Yeah, missed you too, but look who I brought.'

She stood back proudly and smiled as Max greeted his old team of scientists from Camp Eden. Moham took both of Dina's hands in his own.

'Thank you for coming back for us,' he said.

'Oh, Moham! I'm so glad you're with us.'

Zac was next off the plane.

'Everything alright, Max?'

'We're getting there. Shall we go to your office and I can catch you up?'

'Sounds good to me.' Zac glanced behind him. 'Where do you want everyone to go?'

Max looked back at the large group of people disembarking.

'Better send them to the mess hall. There's refreshments available and Layla can assign them to one of the remaining groups ready for travel.'

'Remaining?' Zac frowned. 'Have people already gone?'

'Let's talk in your office.' Max smiled briefly and led the way, Dina happily chatting next to him.

'Hernandez!' Zac called and his lieutenant hurried over. 'Get everyone into the mess hall, see that they have something to eat and drink and wait for me there. I'll come brief everyone soon.'

The base was quiet as they walked through to Zac's office. Although it had never been exactly teeming with people, now they didn't see a single person on the way. Zac was buzzing with questions by the time they arrived at the room and sat down.

'Where is everyone?' he asked just as Max also spoke.

'Where's Artem?'

Before either man could reply, Ash came dashing through the door.

'Sorry, sorry. I missed you at the airstrip. Hi, hi everyone. Where's Artem?'

That made Zac laugh as the others called out hellos to Ash.

'Look, why don't you go first. Then we'll report in,' he suggested, taking a seat.

Lucas was still asleep. Martha held him close as she sat and smiled at Max, waiting to hear what he had to say. Dina sat with her, grinning at her fiancée. Ash took the last chair in the room, ready to chip in if Max needed him to.

Max ran a hand through is hair as he thought about where to begin.

'Have you had any contact with the others?' he asked.

'Briefly,' replied Martha. 'We know they made it to City 50 but that the city has been plagued with 'flu and that the contact, Bridget has died.'

'Yes, she has. The survivors wouldn't let them in initially until they realised it was Jed Jenkins at the gates. Apparently, his mother has some influence in New Corp?'

Martha smiled.

'You could say that.'

'Right, well, they got in to find out that half the city has been lost to a virulent strain of the 'flu. Those that were left were relieved to see them. Sadly, as you know, Bridget Mulherne, the person Zac made the initial agreement with, didn't make it but the people in charge knew the details and Archer has ensured a new agreement has been drawn up, signed and ratified.'

'We have somewhere to go.' Zac sounded relieved.

'Yes. And they are very keen to share the AI and the seed bank. Everyone who arrives has to be inoculated against the 'flu, but I can't see that being a problem.'

There were murmurs of agreement in the room.

'So who's already gone?' asked Zac.

'Almost everyone. Bennett was first with her plants and all non-essential people to help her transport everything. They've safely arrived, and I believe she's telling City 50 exactly what they should be doing.'

'What about the seed bank?' asked Martha. 'It did not seem like it was an easy thing to move. All that security and tech.'

It was Ash who replied this time.

'Bennett is a genius, but don't tell her I said it. When she first designed the seed bank, she made it modular so it could be safely broken down and transported. Each piece a closed circuit of its own, maintaining the environmental conditions the seeds need. It's like she knew it was never going to be a permanent fixture.'

'It's funny really, for someone so against technology, she's actually very technically minded,' agreed Max.

'Who's left then?' Zac was keen to know where they were with the evacuation.

'There's only a couple of teams left. We split up the medics, peacekeepers and techies and each group had a mixture of people. Plus, we staggered their departures, ensuring it wasn't too many people at once on the other end. So far, so good, we haven't had any major accidents and the weather has been on our side.' Max rubbed his hands together. 'There's just the people you brought and like I said, two, possibly three teams left here. The AIs are ready to move. We're good to go.' He looked at Ash to see if he had anything more to add.

'Yeah, we're all packed up. We made the decision to amalgamate the AIs together in an effort to combat the memory loss and retain some of their developed learning. Glover felt it was safer to do that and then make a backup copy as well. Worst-case scenario is they lose their memory of working here but their baseline function will remain. We can rebuild them into separate entities when we get to City 50 if we need to, or we can leave it as one.'

'Huh,' Dina looked sad. 'I never got to say goodbye to Layla.'

'What about you? Where is Artem?' asked Max.

'Artem… he's been working for New Corp,' said Zac.

'But he killed Sean! And now he's captaining a boat with everyone from City 42 and 9,' Dina broke in excitedly.

'He's what?' Max couldn't take it all in. 'Working for

New Corp?'

Martha took over.

'Artem was sharing intelligence with everyone, us and New Corp. It is obviously how he made his money and got his hands on all those supplies. I mean, we all knew he had nefarious dealings, did we not?'

There were reluctant nods. Martha continued.

'We went to his complex first. He wanted to check the safe room, but no-one made it inside.' She looked down at the sleeping boy in her arms. 'We found Ruth and Sarah and we buried them.'

Silent tears fell down Dina's face; Max came and held her in comfort.

'Gaia came and grew a beautiful rose bush for them, in their honour.'

'You saw her?' Max asked.

'No, but the bush grew in front of our eyes, who else could it have been?' Martha had unshed tears in her eyes and took a moment to compose herself before she carried on.

'We were arrested when we arrived at City 42. They tried to take Lucas away, but Zac would not let them.' She smiled gratefully at him. 'That is when Sean revealed Artem had been working for them all along. And that is when we met with Gretchen, Jed's mother.'

'Is she in charge?' Max was intrigued.

'Yes. The leaders of New Corp left on a plane, leaving everyone else behind. To survive or not. I assume they did not come here?' Martha asked.

'No, they didn't make it anywhere.' Ash said with a smile. 'The plane got caught in bad weather and crashed. No survivors. The satellites showed a massive storm epicentre that came out of nowhere and focused on their exact location.'

'Gaia,' breathed Dina.

'Possibly,' agreed Ash. 'I know I should feel sad about the fact that people died but I can't help feeling satisfied that they all perished. After everything they were responsible for.'

'They ordered the destruction of Artem's compound,' added Martha.

'Is that why Artem killed Sean? Wasn't he your aide when you were governor?' asked Max. He was now perched on the arm of Dina's chair so they could be close.

'Oh, you should have seen him. He stretched out his arms and bam, the man was dead. He snapped his neck. Just like that.' Dina couldn't keep the awe out of her words.

Max shook his head and Ash looked shocked.

'Are we sure he's on our side now?' Ash asked.

'He and Gretchen are taking the citizens from 42 down to 9, hoping to convince them to leave and come here on Artem's boat,' replied Zac.

'Artem has a boat?' asked Max.

'Of course he does,' said Martha with a chuckle and they all smiled at that.

'When will they be here? Should we wait for them before we leave?' Max was wondering how much longer they would be delayed.

'They said they would follow on in two days. I don't think we all need to wait for them. Maybe leave behind one final team to help them on their way. Hernandez and Yarrow could head it up. Is Yarrow still here?' Zac glanced around the room.

'Yeah, he was chivvying the last of the techies to pack up once and for all before they leave tomorrow. That's a good idea. They both know the base well and have the authority to marshal the citizens from the island up the mountain but...' Max ran his hand through his hair again. 'I don't have any spare supplies for them. We've packed everything up.'

'Do not worry,' replied Martha. 'Gretchen will make sure the people bring the essentials with them. We gave her the comms link for getting in touch here. We should hear from them tomorrow.'

Zac was nodding.

'I think we should wait for them to get in touch and then evac who we have here, apart from a team to guide the last arrivals up the mountain. Everyone agreed?'

There were nods and murmurs of assent all around.

'Okay. I'm headed to the mess hall to talk to the new arrivals. Max, Ash – come with me?'

Max stood reluctantly. He knew he ought to go with Zac, but he wanted to spend some time with Dina. She stood and entwined her fingers into his.

'Come on, then,' she said, leaning into him. She had no plans to let him out of her sight and if that meant going to a briefing then that's what she was doing.

Chapter Forty

'They're not coming? What, none of them?' Zac was sat in the comms room, speaking to Gretchen in City 9.

'The representatives of the city are adamant that until New Corp give the order, they are going to stay where they are,' she replied.

'Did you explain that you are effectively what's left of New Corp?'

'Of course I did. But they will not recognise my authority. Idiots.' Gretchen looked ruffled and did not have her usual composure. 'They've convinced some of the people from City 42 to also stay.' She sighed. 'We don't have time to do anything about it. We have to accept their decision and leave them behind.'

Zac nodded slowly. He didn't like it, but Gretchen was right.

'Okay, I'll let the others know. We're leaving today for City 50 but there will be a team here to receive you and whoever you bring with you. How's Artem?'

'He's fine, chomping at the bit to be off and away. I expect we will be sailing tonight. There is no point in waiting for people who don't want to come with us.' Gretchen's gaze softened. 'Don't blame yourself, Zachery. You did everything within your power to convince them to leave. Think about the people you were able to save.'

Zac nodded but he couldn't take much comfort in her words.

'We'll see you at 50 then,' he said.

'At 50. Take care.' And Gretchen signed off.

Zac sighed and pushed his chair away from the comms screen. All those people were going to die and there was nothing he could do about it. Slowly he stood up to go find the others and tell them the bad news.

'Idiots!' said Dina, echoing Gretchen's sentiment.

Martha was more resigned.

'We did everything we could. If they do not want to listen to the truth, then…' she shrugged. 'Are we still leaving today?'

'I see no reason to wait,' replied Zac. 'Are you all packed?'

'Yep, we're packed up and Ash has gone to get his sister. There's about twenty of us in total, the last few people from tech and some peacekeepers,' replied Max. 'Shall we meet at the north entrance in say, half an hour? I'll spread the word.'

'Sounds good,' said Zac and watched Dina and Max hurry off to tell the others. 'Can I help with anything?' He turned to Martha.

'No. We are pretty much sorted. Max made sure Frank held back some baby supplies for us and I have been able to restock everything. We are good to go.' She smiled at him. 'Do you fancy a synth-caf? If you are not needed elsewhere.'

'I'd love one.'

Zac held out his hand, and after a moment's hesitation, Martha took it and they smiled at each other as they ambled along the corridor to the mess hall, pushing Lucas along in front of them.

Chapter Forty-One

'When will they get here?' asked Kira. She was both excited at seeing her friends again and nervous that they hadn't arrived yet.

'Ash said they were on track to arrive early this afternoon so not long.' Jed smiled at his wife. It was good to see her getting excited about something. She'd really struggled with her grief over the loss of Ruth, Sarah and her parents, but she seemed to be coming out the other side. Her sunny nature was returning.

'And they all have somewhere assigned to live, haven't they?'

'You know they have, hon. You drilled Monique to make sure we all got houses together, remember?'

'I know but I want everything to be perfect for when they arrive.' Kira grinned at her husband. 'Can you feel it? Everything is going to be alright; I just know it.'

'Shall we go and wait down by the gates? Then we can see them arrive,' suggested Jed.

Opening the gates had been one of the first things the new arrivals had tackled. The remaining citizens of City 50 had been vehemently against it, frightened that they would be plagued with another deadly illness. It had taken several days of convincing before the council had finally agreed to open the gates, but they insisted that all new arrivals came through decontamination before entering the city proper.

There was a small garden inside the gates and the children pottered about on the grass, squealing with excitement at every leaf they found. Kira and Jed sat on the grass and watched the empty path in front of them. They didn't have to wait long.

'Kira!' It was Dina, grinning like mad. 'Jed! It's so great to see you guys. We've made it!' She hugged them both then bent down to say hi to Grace and Peter.

Max was next, heading up the caravan of people and supplies.

'Hi guys, where do you want us?'

More people had come out of City 50 and were helping to unload the supplies.

'Everyone needs to go through decontamination then Monique will gather everyone's name and speciality, then we can get you settled in,' explained Jed.

'Sounds easy enough,' commented Max.

'We've had plenty of practice,' laughed Kira. 'Are you the last group? Where's Martha and Lucas? And Zac?'

'They're bringing up the rear,' said Dina. She bent closer to Kira. 'I think they've finally got together.'

The two women grinned at each other and started gossiping about the budding relationship as they walked towards the decontamination entrance.

'Are you coming through?' Max asked Jed.

'No, we've been done. I think Kira wants to wait for Martha, so we'll hang on.'

'Have you heard from your mother?'

Jed smiled.

'She, my father and Artem landed yesterday with

everyone they could convince to come. She's not wasting any time and they're starting the journey up today. It won't take them long. Between her and Artem, I don't think anyone else gets a say.'

Max laughed.

'You're probably right.' He clapped a hand on Jed's shoulder. 'See you on the other side.'

Kira came back to Jed and held his hand.

'We're all going to be together again soon,' she said.

'Yep. Shouldn't be long.' Jed looked out at more new people arriving then pointed. 'Isn't that them?'

Kira squinted and then squeezed her husband's hand in excitement. She waved wildly and it wasn't long before Martha and Zac noticed her and waved back.

'You made it!' gushed Kira, giving Martha a hug.

'Yes, we are here.' She looked tired but happy.

'How has the agreement with City 50 been?' asked Zac, wasting no time with pleasantries.

'It's been fine. They seem thrilled to have us and of course the seed back and AIs were a big sell for them.' Jed looked round at the milling people. 'Between all of us, we have everything we need to not just survive but to build a future.'

'That is good to hear,' said Martha. 'Why is everyone queuing?'

'Oh, that's the decontamination. It doesn't take long, but they won't let you in without it. And I can't blame them, they've suffered a massive loss,' explained Kira. 'We'll wait with you.' And she linked arms with Martha as they walked over to the moving line.

'You heard about what happened with Artem?' Zac asked Jed as they waited.

'Sounds like he came down firmly on our side in the end.'

'Yeah, I guess. Where's Archer?' Zac asked.

'She's on the inside, marshalling the new arrivals and getting them settled in the right quadrants in the city. Ash has been working with Monique, City 50's admin clerk, to work out assignments based on individual strengths and the housing has been mixed up so there's no divide between old and new citizens.'

'Sounds like you have it all under control.' Zac was impressed.

'Hmm.'

'Something wrong?'

'We have no real governance in place. The council wants to wait until Mother arrives before they will consider forming a proper government. They seem to think she speaks with the authority of New Corp.' Jed glanced at Zac. 'What do you think?'

'New Corp is gone. But she is probably the highest ranking official from the organisation. So, it makes sense that they'd want to wait for her, but I wouldn't worry. I doubt she's going to suggest we reform. Coming here to City 50 is all about a new beginning.'

'I hope you're right.'

The queue had almost ended.

'I'll see you in there,' said Jed and he waved goodbye at Zac, Martha and Lucas before herding Kira and his kids back into the city.

Once everyone was through decontamination it was time for a reunion. Ash, Glover, Archer, Simmonds and Kolwowsky joined Kira and Jed in officially welcoming Dina, Max, Martha, and Zac to City 50.

They all met in Kira and Jed's assigned house. The children were put to bed in their shared cube, glad to be reunited. Ash produced a bottle of vodka to cheers from the others and he poured out the shots.

'Where's Bennett?' asked Max, looking around.

'She's grilling Moham and the others from Camp Eden. She was really excited to see their research and samples. We can catch up with them tomorrow.' Ash handed Max a shot and made sure everyone else had one. 'To our future,' he toasted.

'To our future!'

After the shots were downed, no-one really knew what to say next.

'What happens now?' asked Martha, breaking the silence.

'We wait for Gretchen, Artem and the others to arrive and then the council have called a meeting to figure out how to move forward,' said Jed.

'And when will they be here?'

'Day after tomorrow.'

'Which means,' interrupted Kira, 'that you can all explore City 50 tomorrow and get a feel for the place. I think you're going to like it.' Her smile was infectious.

Ash went around with the vodka again.

'To City 50!' he proposed, and the others echoed his toast loudly.

'It feels almost too good to be true,' said Martha quietly, her mood sombre. 'We have been through so much, lost so much. It is difficult to imagine we have actually got to the end. Or the beginning, if you know what I mean.'

'I do.' Kira gave her friend a hug. 'This is the beginning of good things.' She held out her glass to Ash for another shot. 'To new beginnings!'

'To new beginnings!'

Chapter Forty-Two

'Come on, we don't want to be late,' called Jed as Kira rushed around trying to sort out the children before they left for the council meeting.

'I know, I know, but I want to make sure they have something to eat. I don't know how long this meeting is going to go on for. Here, shove that in the bag. I'm ready.' She handed him a packet of snacks then scooped up first Grace then Peter and put them in the stroller.

They hurried out of their house, across the square to the council building and quickly went in. They had to wait at the security desk as their identities were cross-checked and they were finally given permission to go through.

'Which meeting room is it?' asked Kira.

'The largest one, at the end of the corridor. Come on.'

As they arrived, Jed pushed the door open for Kira and she went through to be met with a room full of people. They all turned to stare at her arrival making her blush and falter.

'Good, good, you're here. We can start. Take your seats everyone,' said Richard, the City 50 council member.

Kira took a seat next to Martha so the children could play quietly in the corner. Jed, Zac, Dina and Max joined them with Archer, Bennett and Glover sitting on the other side of the table next to Gretchen and Artem. Olive and Liss were there as well as Dr Lee from City 42 and of course, Monique.

Richard stayed standing and coughed to get everyone's attention.

'Thank you all for coming. It's been a funny few days, what with the new arrivals and our city back to full capacity. Exciting times ahead I'm sure, but what you've all been called to today is a breakdown of how city rule will happen in the future. I'm sure I don't need to remind you all that without law and order, a city cannot function, there needs to be someone in charge. I suggest that we learn from the lessons of those who came before us and vote in a governing council. One that will have the best interests of the city at its heart.' He gestured to Monique, who was sat next to him. 'Monique has, as you know, been classifying all the new arrivals according to their strengths and abilities so that we can assign individuals to roles where they will be useful members of society, and with some careful guidance at our end, I feel sure that each and every person can be moulded into the perfect citizen. Now, before you came and before we were incapacitated by the 'flu, New Corp had provided neural implants designed to keep citizens compliant and aggression free. I see no reason why we cannot continue that agenda and roll out those devices. There are lots of new people, it is naïve to think there would be no friction.' He paused for breath but before he could continue, Kira stood up.

'No. This is all wrong. Don't you see?' She looked imploringly around the table. 'This is not how we are meant to live. Neural implants to keep citizens compliant? Carrying out New Corp's agenda when there isn't even any New Corp left? It's insane. We already know those mistakes. It's time to move on. We need to permanently open the gates, break down our barriers and live with nature, not against it. It's the only way we can survive.'

'But it's not safe out there,' protested Olive.

'It's not safe anywhere! If you lock us up in this city, we'll diminish and die off. What about the cities we couldn't get in touch with? What if there are more survivors out there?' Kira glanced at Jed who gave her a nod of encouragement and she carried on. 'There's a whole world out there and we've been guided to this place of safety to live through the environmental crisis because the planet still needs us, she still wants us to be a part of her world. We need to honour her, not shut her out.'

Richard threw his hands up in the air.

'What exactly should we do then?'

'Keep an open mind. Don't shut yourself away from the world or the wonders of nature that lie behind these gates. We can learn from our mistakes; I know we can.'

There was a long silence as no-one said anything. Eventually Gretchen cleared her throat and spoke.

'I agree with Kira. For too long we have hidden behind our walls. Corporation, New Corp, whatever you want to call it, no longer exists. For the first time in a long time, we are free citizens. I vote no to the implants. If you agree, raise your hand.'

Everyone apart from Richard lifted their hand, and when he realised he was the only one who hadn't, he grew flustered.

'It's not that I don't agree with you, we just need to

be able to, I don't know, control the population somehow. We can't have lawlessness and a free for all. You must see that.' He sat down and crossed his arms.

'We won't.' This time it was Zac who spoke. He gestured around the room. 'You have a wealth of experience right here in this room, plus all the different knowledge from all the citizens out there in the city. Now is not the time to silence them.' He stood up and pointed at Martha, then Gretchen. 'You have two previous city governors, right here. Artem, Jed, Archer and I have experience in safeguarding populations, we have military training, ideal to run a peacekeeping operation. You have Dr Bennett and Dr Carter, experts in their fields of botany, plus a team of scientists dedicated to improving plant yield and of course the seed bank.' He kept walking around the table. 'You have Ash, Dr Glover and her team of technicians, all constantly working on new tech and the AIs are here to help improve everyone's lives. This is Dr Lee, former head of Medical in City 42 – he can ensure the health and well-being of all our citizens are looked after.' He came back round to Kira's chair and put his hands on the back of it. 'Lastly, and most importantly, we have the wealth and experience of mothers, of all the people who've risked everything to get here, to this point. Let's draw on all of those things and build a better future.'

'We have to be honest with each other. We have to learn how to live with our planet in harmony and look after everyone to the best of our ability.' Kira surveyed the room. 'I know we can do it.'

There were faint murmurs of agreements and a few nods as the people in the room looked around at each other and realised that they were the architects of their future.

Kira's attention was distracted by a small movement in the window. As she glanced over, she saw the faintest outline of a blue goddess smiling through at them all. Kira beamed back. Her confidence full she turned her focus back to the meeting and organising the new council of survivors.

~The End~

Thank You

Thank you for reading The Gaia Solution, I really hope you enjoyed reading the third and final instalment to The Gaia Collection. I would be so grateful if you could review the book on Amazon and Goodreads and let me know what you thought.

Cover artist Ian Bristow has once again stepped up the plate and created a wonderful book cover for me. I'm sure you'll agree how well the series covers fit together.

I want to say a special thank you to my wonderful team of beta readers - Donna Tyrrell, Debbie McGowan and Martin Frowd. Your comments and feedback were excellent, and I am thrilled that I brought you to tears lol.

I couldn't write without my fabulous husband, Kevin, so a huge thank you to him. And to my incredibly patient children, Leo (6) and Anabelle (2) who don't really understand why but let Mummy do her 'work' on the laptop while they play lego.

About the Author

Claire Buss is a multi-genre author and poet based in the UK. She wanted to be Lois Lane when she grew up but work experience at her local paper was eye-opening. Instead, Claire went on to work in a variety of admin roles for over a decade but never felt quite at home. An avid reader, baker and Pinterest addict Claire won second place in the Barking and Dagenham Pen to Print writing competition in 2015 with her debut novel, The Gaia Effect, setting her writing career in motion. She continues to write passionately and is hopelessly addicted to cake.

Sign up to Claire's newsletter for exclusive content and all the latest writing news: http://eepurl.com/c93M2L

Follow Claire on Twitter: @grasshopper2407
Like Claire on Facebook: facebook.com/busswriter
Visit her website: www.cbvisions.weebly.com

The Rose Thief

Ned Spinks, Chief Thief-Catcher has a problem. Someone is stealing the Emperor's roses. But that's not the worst of it. In his infinite wisdom and grace, the Emperor magically imbued his red rose with love so if it was ever removed from the Imperial Rose Gardens then love will be lost, to everyone, forever. It's up to Ned and his band of motley catchers to apprehend the thief and save the day. But the thief isn't exactly who they seem to be, neither is the Emperor. Ned and his team will have to go on a quest defeating vampire mermaids, illusionists, estranged family members and an evil sorcerer in order to win the day. What could possibly go wrong?

This award-winning humorous fantasy novel is available at your favourite retailer, so get your copy today!